A CALL TO POWER:
THE GRANDMOTHERS SPEAK

———⋙•◦•⋘———

Finding Balance in a Chaotic World

By

Sharon McErlane

Net of Light Press
www.grandmothersspeak.com

Published by Net of Light Press, 9/9/06
www.grandmothersspeak.com

ISBN: 0-9788468-0-X
ISBN - 13: 978-0-9788468-0-0

Originally published by Author House, 4/23/04
ISBN: 1-4140-5316-9(e-book), ISBN: 1-4184-3946-5(paperback)

Library of Congress Control Number for first edition:
2003099486

Cover Art: Francene Hart, www.francenehart.com
Cover Design: Sirius Graphics, Tim Brittain
Illustrations: Sharon McErlane

Printed in the United States of America by Net Pub press

Copies of this book are available through Net of Light Press at
www.grandmothersspeak.com

"When the wisdom of the Grandmothers
is heard, the world will heal."
—*Native American prophecy*

CONTENTS

ACKNOWLEDGEMENTS

A Call to Power: The Grandmothers Speak has not been an easy book to write, mainly because of my reoccurring thoughts of unworthiness. Thoughts that asked over and over again, "Who do you think you are to convey material like this?" Many times I became overwhelmed by the task before me, and if it had not been for the following people I might have given it up. From the bottom of my heart I thank Lori Viera, Steven Atherton, Katie McMahaon, Pat Durkin, Mahri Kintz, Meinrad Craighead, Dorothy Herrin, Jim Farris, Dyan Ellerbrach, Richard Carlson, Sheryl Politiski, Benjamin Shields, Susan Sherman, Deborah Schmidt, and Christan Hummel.

I also thank the women who brought the Grandmothers' book, message and me to the wonderful country of Lithuania. Thank you Antanina, Vilma, Ritone and Susie.

For the lovely artwork, cover design and layout of this revised edition, I wish to thank Tim Brittain and Francene Hart. They have added so much to the new "look" of this book.

And lastly to my beloved husband Roger, without whose support I would never have been able to do this work.

The Grandmothers have come at this time to lift humanity and fill our hearts with light so that we in turn can hold our beloved planet in light. The above-mentioned people helped launch this book, making it possible for others to then pass the Grandmothers' message of light and joy throughout the world. This book is dedicated to each of them and to the Divine (in all its radiant forms) working with and through them.

Thank you, Grandmothers, for making all this possible.

FOREWORD

A Call to Change

The Grandmothers appeared in my life uninvited, although they and the message they brought became most welcome. They came literally from out of the blue, and placing me in situations that were foreign to me, they changed my life. They have come to correct the imbalance of yin and yang on our planet and awaken women and men to the energy of what they call "the deep feminine." To give both men and women an intimate connection with the Feminine Principle of creation.

Their purpose is to bring women and men, yin and yang into balance with one another. I am more grateful than I can say to be part of their work and have this opportunity to pass on their wisdom.

The Grandmothers convey their message, demonstrate the changes taking place on earth, explain why our world is in a dangerous state, and tell us what we can do to help ourselves and our planet regain balance. Their meditations and visualizations enable everyone to connect with one another. At this time a powerful human connection provides a web or net of yin support for the planet, holding the earth steady while the necessary changes in its energy field take place.

The Grandmothers explain this imbalance and demonstrate the difference between masculine and feminine energy. They teach us how to move into a closer, more personal relationship with the Divine and encourage us to imbue our lives with the presence of the Sacred. You may choose to return several times to the meditations at the end of the book in order to implement them more powerfully in your life.

Some will read this book for information and some will read for self-transformation. Some will be comfortable hearing about the Grandmothers while others will want to experience them. The exercises or meditations at the end of the book are for those who seek self-transformation and/or a personal relationship with these wise women.

Because the energy imbalance on earth has existed for so long, the Grandmothers say that today we are in desperate straits. Yet because the process of correcting this imbalance has already begun, the earth will not be destroyed. You will find the Grandmothers' message profound and uplifting, and although this is a serious book it is not a gloomy one.

A Call to Power: the Grandmothers Speak can be read on many levels. It can be, for you, a true-life story, an explanation of a new way of living, an invitation to enter into that life, a personal journey, or a myth. At different times in your life it can be all of these. I know that everything I relate within its pages took place, yet I invite you to read it from whatever viewpoint is best for you. There is value in each view.

This is particularly a book for women. It calls a woman to power, gives her an understanding of the nature of yin, and gives her tools to apply its power. Since yin energy exists in all beings, *A Call to Power: the Grandmothers Speak* is at the same time a book for men. It gives men an appreciation of the Feminine Principle and awakens them to this nurturing and supportive quality within themselves. The Grandmothers' book provides a framework for understanding the changes taking place on earth and teaches us how to take part in the sacred evolution of our planet.

The Grandmothers invite us to participate in restoring harmony to earth; however, they assure us that our participation in this work is optional, not essential. Righting the balance on earth will take place whether or not we participate. "We give you this opportunity for your own sake," they say, "because participating in this work will bring you joy." (The bold print throughout the book denotes the Grandmother's words, and even when they are speaking to me, their messages are meant for all.)

The Grandmothers speak and live TRUTH. Right from the first they thrilled and shocked me with their unexpected lessons. Master teachers, they surprised me from the moment I met them—that innocent September morning when I walked the dog along the cliff above the beach.

CHAPTER 1

A Visit from the Grandmothers

"In order to confirm woman from within herself the Great Council of the Grandmothers has come."

It was a seemingly normal fall day. I was just going for a walk. Another clear September morning, it was early, about seven o'clock, and I had taken the dog with me. With the summer tourists gone, the town was quiet again, peaceful.

The stillness that lay over the town was as reflective as I. For days I had been thinking about the direction of my life's work, and as I mulled this over once again the dog pulled on the leash, hurrying me across Pacific Coast Highway toward the beach. We were approaching the walkway along the cliff when a group of older women suddenly appeared in front of us. It was the oddest thing. They were simply there.

The women gathered around us, speaking and gesturing with great animation, and as they smiled and laughed with one another, they beckoned me to join them. Their voices rang round me as they called to each other and for a moment I caught a bit of a song they were singing. With gleeful, girlish laughter they bunched themselves in close to me.

They were lovely, welcoming and so happy; I immediately noticed their sweet, open faces. But when they stood close I saw that they wore costumes from distant times and places. I stared, open mouthed, while I tried to make sense of this, but one with long gray hair fixed me with such a welcoming smile that for a moment I forgot about their strangeness.

Then I noticed that I was looking *through* them. I could see trees, the walkway to the beach and the waves of the ocean right through their bodies. I shook my head, trying to clear my vision but they were still transparent. Could this be a dream?

As I continued to stare, I realized that I could smell the air from the sea and feel the wet grass and the cracks of the sidewalk underneath my sandals. Just then a neighbor who walks at the same time I do each morning waved and spoke to me and automatically I responded. "Oh, my God," I thought. I was caught in a double reality. This was a *spiritual* experience, a vision. I was having a vision!

My mouth got dry, I broke into a sweat and quickly I tried to dismiss these old women. This must be my imagination—right? What else could it be? I must be making the whole thing up and they would go away in a minute. I had never seriously thought I might be crazy before but this...

As the vision or whatever it was continued my mouth got drier and I noticed I was holding my breath. What was happening to me was far beyond my understanding and though I wanted to flee from the strangeness of it, I was too fascinated. I couldn't take my eyes off these women. And their soft smiles let me know that they understood my dilemma. Those smiles and the air of patience they wore helped me maintain some equilibrium. As they watched me deal with my fear they nodded, smiled all the more and simply waited, and because they behaved the way they did I was able to stop my fear from escalating.

Then the thought came that what I was seeing was real. Visions aren't something the mind manufactures. Visions are just another form of reality—emanations of energy, like everything else. These thoughts moved through my mind in an instant, surprising me. But the emanations of energy standing in front of me weren't ones I was used to and I was frightened.

I tried to flee from these women but they were persistent and stayed with me as I continued my walk. A group of grandmotherly-looking women who, in spite of my best efforts to ignore them, continued to embrace and talk to me. I had to pay attention to them because although their presence wasn't physical, it was undeniable. And they wouldn't go away.

Finally I stopped fighting the experience and gave them my full attention. That's when I noticed that two of them were dressed in beaded deerskin dresses and leggings. Native Americans in full regalia!

Another woman especially stood out from the group. She was quite a bit taller than the others; her Negroid features and elegant head rose high above theirs and her long neck was stacked with bronze necklaces. She looked like a picture from an old National Geographic I had seen as a child. Her sculpted face and regal bearing marked her for a queen from an ancient African civilization.

Several women were less than five feet tall and almost square in shape. Brown skin and long, gray-brown hair worn loose over their shoulders, they were clothed in primitive looking dresses like gunny-sacks. Made of fibrous material these hung on them just as a sack or bag would. Because their skin and dresses were the same color the only thing that enlivened their appearance were strands of brightly colored beads and shells hanging around their necks. They looked like tribal women from southern Mexico or Guatemala. I stared at them, wondering what they were doing in this resort town but they smiled back at me, smiles of such sweetness and confidence that before I knew it I smiled back. My fear was melting.

Three or four were draped in robes of muted grays, blues and mauves that had a Biblical look. Their hair was covered by a hood or cape but I could see by their fair skin that they were of European origin. There were others too.

As they smiled, called to me, and opened their arms, welcoming me into their midst, I felt they were delighted to see me. Stroking my face and patting me on the shoulders and back they put their arms around me and gathering me in, formed a circle with me inside.

I counted around a dozen grouped around me and knew somehow that together they represented all the races of humankind. They were queenly and as this thought came to me one of them spoke. **"Each woman is in her own way, beautiful and wise,"** she said. **"And although each of us is unique in her power and being, all of us are as one in our purpose."** Together they announced, **"We are the Great Council of the Grandmothers."** I was awed, impressed not only by the grandeur of their presence, but by their name too. " The Council of the Grandmothers" fit them perfectly, as imposing and dignified as they were.

They would sometimes appear to me like this. But over the following years I would meet with them hundreds of times in different guises.

Now they invited me into their midst and with soft touches and penetrating looks into my eyes, held and embraced me. As this drama played on, I still walked the dog and greeted my neighbors. Somehow my consciousness was overlapping in a seamless way. It had placed me in two realities at the same time. I walked along and the Grandmothers talked to me, my neighbors greeted me the way they did every morning, while the dog tugged on the leash. I responded to them all.

Being involved in two seemingly separate realities gave me an odd, disoriented feeling, but surprisingly, it was not difficult to navigate like this. At one point I almost laughed out loud at the absurdity of my situation. But strangely enough, I also felt peaceful and somehow lifted by the energy of these Grandmothers.

Holding me close, they said, **"Plant your feet firmly in the soft dusty soil of Mother earth."** Their choice of words and their distinctive tone got my attention. I stopped walking and thought of my feet, not on the pavement, but on the earth and immediately from above my head a cocoon of glowing silk folded down over me. Many yards long, at least six feet wide, it vibrated with the color of a glorious sunset, a dusty rose that seemed to glow with a life of its own.

I drew in a long breath as the cascade enveloped me. It felt so comforting. As the Grandmothers wrapped and covered me with it they announced, **"This is a caul. The caul is formed of a substance like light but more than light."** Its silkiness against my skin gave me the understanding that yes, it was light, light with heft or body.

It covered me from head to toe, cocooned me. **"This caul will begin to heal and nourish you from the skin side in, soaking through the cells and organs of your body and aligning and harmonizing all of your parts together. A healing and awakening is now beginning which will take place within you on all levels, simultaneously. Your physical, mental, emotional, and spiritual aspects will receive what they need; they will heal, and harmonize together."** As they spoke I felt more deeply nourished and cared for than I could remember.

Still covering me with this envelope of silk, they gently rocked, then danced me. Holding me out in front of them, raising my hands, they lifted me up, whirled me around, and laughing all the while, made me feel like a small child who is greatly loved. Next they taught me how to step with them, step back and forth and side to side. In this way we danced together. As they embraced me again, I thought, "This is all so wonderful, but what can I give back to them?" Though I didn't speak the thought, they replied, **"Do not to do anything now. Do not to try to help us. But instead, let us do all the giving and all the work."** I took them at their word and let myself relax into their care.

I came home from that walk full of wonder at what had happened to me and although I didn't understand it, I knew I wasn't crazy. I was too peaceful and happy for that. Dazed, I sat down on the couch and wrote what came to me; I wanted to keep the magic of the morning alive. Then I put away my writing. I didn't even read it. I didn't want to.

I had heard about experiences like this, been told about their preciousness and fragility. I also understood that it is the nature of the mind to attempt to explain and reduce every experience into something it can categorize. But what had happened to me could not be categorized and I decided not to try. Instead I would stay present in the moment, not look back to what had happened on that walk and not speculate on what it might mean. What had taken place was sacred, that I knew, and for now that would be enough.

I hummed with a special kind of happiness a long time after that morning and wanting to keep it that way I told no one about what had happened to me. I felt about my experience the way I might about a bottle of expensive perfume. I wanted to keep the stopper closed, not dilute what was in the bottle. Besides, explaining what had happened would require more energy and clarity than I had.

I knew I had been given a gift, and this gift needed to be honored and hidden away in silence. The Grandmothers had said that the healing and nourishing work of the caul would soak into me, and that's exactly what I wanted it to do.

Before meeting the Grandmothers the only time I had heard the word "caul" used was to describe the amniotic sack that covers some babies at birth. I didn't know what the Grandmothers meant by the word but whatever had covered and wrapped me had made me feel cherished. I wanted it to soak into me so deeply that I would feel wrapped in love like that forever.

Some time later, I don't remember when, I happened across "caul," and the meaning given for it was "initiation." I was surprised and yet not as I read "initiation," because at some level I knew this was what I had received. The caul had transmitted a particular energy to my body and mind, and I had felt it strongly—a peaceful strength, a sense of inner wealth I had never known before. This feeling stayed with me for several weeks. Strangely, however, when I later searched for the word, caul, I never found this meaning again. Perhaps the definition of the caul as initiation came to me in a dream.

Another startling visitation occurred around this time. I was walking up the hall stairs while I waited for a client, when I glanced out the back window and saw an enormous bird of prey sitting on our garden stepladder. Bigger than any hawk I had ever seen, he perched on that four-foot ladder, his size and bearing so out of place that he dwarfed not only the ladder, but also the entire quarter acre of garden. Dark gray-brown feathers, he had piercing eyes, and just perched there, not hunting, not roosting, and turning his head in a full circle he fiercely guarded the garden.

My husband and I couldn't take our eyes off him and when my client arrived, I showed her the bird too. I was so grateful that others were there to see this with me. I still hadn't told anyone about the Grandmothers. We watched the great bird in fascination, but we finally looked away, and when we turned back, he was gone. None of us had seen him land or fly off.

A few days later Roger and I mentioned our garden visitor to a birder. Excited by our description, especially by the bird's size, she brought out a copy of Floyd Scholtz's *Birds of Prey*. We found it. He had been a golden eagle—a raptor extremely rare in the densely populated part of southern California where we live.

After we identified our garden visitor I took out the Medicine Cards, a system of instruction and divination from Native American teaching, and looked up the eagle totem. Eagle is the first card of the deck, which told me something. Gazing at the card I felt again the thrill of the great bird's presence. I read, "Eagle medicine is the power of the Great Spirit, the connection to the Divine. It is the ability to live in the realm of spirit, and yet remain connected and balanced within the realm of Earth."*

A familiar chill, the recognition of truth, shot downward, then climbed back up my spine. "Eagle is reminding you to take heart and gather your courage, for the universe is presenting you with an opportunity to soar above the mundane levels of your life. The power of recognizing this opportunity may come in the form of a spiritual test. In learning to fiercely attack your personal fear of the unknown, the wings of your soul will be supported by the ever present breezes which are the breath of the Great Spirit."

With these words ringing true, I recognized that the universe *was* presenting me with an unimagined opportunity. If I were to accept it I would be operating outside the bounds of my "mundane life."

Around the first of October I was rummaging in my desk and remembered to look at what I had written the day the Grandmothers appeared to me. I was stunned by what was on the page.

"With culture so long dominated by yang, the principle of masculine energy, yin, the principle of feminine energy, has become deficient and weak. Woman is cut off from her own sense of power and purpose, which comprise her beauty, and feeling this lack, she seeks outer confirmation of her identity and worth. Women spend inordinate amounts of time and money in order to be confirmed from without.

"No matter how many 'confirmations' of her beauty, her power and purpose, she receives, yet she feels the lack. This is because feminine energy cannot be conferred from the outside. Yin is. It exists for its own sake. Seeking it will only confuse the seeker.

"In order to confirm woman from within herself and awaken man to the comforting presence within himself, the Great Council of the Grandmothers has come. Each Grandmother is unique in her power and being and yet all are as One in this purpose—to restore

yin, the feminine energy, to full beauty/power so that the world may once again come into balance. We will empower women and comfort men, awakening them both to the feminine principle."

It was in my handwriting, yet I had no memory of writing it. I realized that the message had been written through me, not by me. I also understood that what I was reading was not for me alone. The truth reverberating in their words was for all women, for all people.

Their words confirmed what I had already known. The world *was* dangerously out of balance. The level of human pain seemed to be rising. I was seeing more suffering from violence and despair in my psychotherapy practice. What the Grandmothers were calling, **"Too much yang and not enough yin,"** was also pushing the nations of the world closer to war. Later on in my work with them, the Grandmothers told me, **"Yin and yang are out of balance. Yang has grown excessive. Increasingly wild and violent, yang energy cannot come back into balance without the intervention of yin."**

In mid-October Roger and I had an appointment with an astrologer. I had finally told him about my experience with the Grandmothers and we were both curious as to whether the astrologer would pick up on this strange happening.

Reading my chart first, Dorothy announced that I was about to begin the work I was born to do—something different from anything I had ever done, intensely spiritual work that would be important to me and to others. She said I must trust in what would be given to me and move forward into this work in full faith. What was being presented was the opportunity of my lifetime.

With a lump in my throat I listened and when I told her about the Grandmothers and the eagle she laughed delightedly and said *this was it!* I would pass the Grandmothers' work on to many women; I would travel and write a book! My chart showed me spending long hours at the computer.

Although Dorothy had been right about many things, she wasn't always right. I was no writer; I had never touched a computer and didn't want to. Roger laughed aloud when she said I would spend long hours at the computer. He knew my phobia of machines

But she wasn't budging. I would teach the Grandmothers' work, I would travel and I would write. Chuckling, she told me to call her and let her know how things were going.

Later, as I began my work with the Grandmothers, her words sustained me. I kept reminding myself that I was to trust what I was being given, knowing I would never forgive myself if I surrendered to my fear of venturing into the unknown. I had to trust the process and go where I was being led. I made a vow then not to give in to my fears but to instead keep focusing within, listening to my heart—no matter what.

The first week in November I attended a painting workshop with Meinrad Craighead, a Benedictine nun, artist and scholar who teaches the art of the Sacred. Here I was introduced to concepts new to me—the feminine aspect of God, the sacred art of the Goddess culture, and shamanism. Confiding in Meinrad what had happened to me in September, I asked her, were the Grandmothers and the eagle connected? She thought so. The visit of the Grandmothers and the eagle followed a classic pattern found in many myths, she said. She encouraged me to find out why they had come.

When I returned home I searched my day planner, looking for the date the eagle had landed in the garden. It was September 12, 1996. Then I pulled out what I had written when the Grandmothers appeared. It was dated September 10. After a lifetime of nothing even remotely like this happening to me, *two visitations had come two days apart.*

Now I really questioned why the Grandmothers and the eagle had appeared. What did they want? But I had no idea how to find out. To ask them I needed a way to contact them and although I waited expectantly for them to return, they didn't. If I wanted to talk to the Grandmothers—I didn't dream of talking to the eagle—I would have to find a way.

I didn't know where to turn for help so I did the only thing I knew— prayed for someone who could help me. I had only done this a few days when, walking through town one morning, I ran into a friend I hadn't seen in a long time. Susan had been in chronic pain for as long as I had known her but today, smiling and confident as she approached me, she radiated health and well-being! When I asked what had happened to her, she told me that for the past few months she had been working with a shaman. This work had made a tremendous difference in her health and attitude.

I was thrilled to see her looking so well but didn't think much about what she had said until the next afternoon when I talked to another friend who mentioned that she too was working with a shaman. Both women were seeing the same one! In my prayers I had asked to be guided to someone who could help me. Maybe this shaman was the person.

*Medicine Cards, the *Discovery of Power through the Ways of Animals*, Jamie Sams & David Carson, Bear & Co., Santa Fe, New Mexico.

CHAPTER 2

We are Bringing to Earth Something of the Sky

The shaman turned out to be a former Catholic nun who had come to California from Mexico only a few years ago. She didn't seem at all exotic the way I had imagined a shaman would, only kind and perceptive. With her friendly face and ready laugh, she reminded me of someone I might run into at the local supermarket.

After listening to my request, she offered to teach me how to journey to levels of what she called "non-ordinary reality" where I might find what I was looking for. I could journey to this world of spirit by listening to the monotonous beat of a drum. This would put me into a light trance.

I was a little bit thrilled and a lot scared by her offer but if I wanted to find these Grandmothers I had to do something. She had a sweet expression, and a lively sense of humor. I decided I would trust her.

This work, she cautioned, was not for everyone, but if I was successful and the Grandmothers met with me, I would have a chance to learn the answers to my questions. I must word my questions clearly so I would know exactly what they were responding to. She would tape record my journey so I could give this adventure my full attention and not worry about remembering it. "You can only try, the rest is up to them," she said, and motioning me to lie down, she turned on the tape.

Trembling with excitement and fear, I lay on her floor. I was to find a place from which to enter what she called the "upper world" where beings like the Grandmothers reside. Here I must "journey," seeking them for as long as the steady beat of the drum continued. When it stopped and changed to a fast beat, I was to begin my return. "Take note," she said, "of the route you travel, and return the same way. Under no circumstance are you to deviate from this procedure." I saw the look she gave me and understood. If I got lost, I might not be able to find my way back.

Now I was really scared. Quickly she covered my eyes with a scarf and as soon as I heard the drum, I prayed hard, straining to remember her directions. First I must find a place from which to enter the upper world. As soon as this thought came a tree I love came to mind. It would be my entry point.

I focused on the tree and suddenly I stood beside it. Turning toward the trunk, then scrambling up its branches, I perched with my head sticking out of the topmost twigs and peered into the expanse above me. I asked for help, bounced on the branch and willed it to spring me into the endless blue above. Amazingly it did and I found myself rising effortlessly into the sky. As soon as the thought came to rise, my body was catapulted skyward. This was already a different sort of reality.

I flew straight into the firmament, enjoying myself immensely until I became aware of a heavy blanket of clouds above me, thick and ominous. How would I get through them? But no sooner did I ask for help than a passageway appeared in the clouds and, with only a little effort on my part, pushing hard with my feet to thrust myself upward while my hands grasped at the formless edges of clouds, I passed through.

I had entered the realm of non-ordinary reality. Here was what the shaman called the first level of the upper world and here I would begin my search for the Grandmothers. Now I was to ask everyone I met, no matter how strange they might appear, if they were my spirit helpers. If they were in fact there to help, I could ask where I might find the Grandmothers.

When I passed through the opening in the clouds I found myself in empty space, blank and devoid of life. No form, no movement, no color, only white space stretched before me. In my mind I called it "the white land."

Because there was no life, no form of any kind here, I would have to go higher to find the Grandmothers. "Please," I pleaded with the universe, "take me to a helping spirit so I can find them."

As soon as the request formed I was lifted from this lifeless space into an arena of blues and whites where clouds, winds and shifting movements were all about. Quickly the colors grew dim, making it dark, then darker still until all I could see was a pair of white eyes staring out of the blackness at me.

"Are you my helping spirit?" I asked the eyes. "Can you take me to the Grandmothers?"

Silence. There was no response, but something behind those eyes beckoned and I followed onward, upward and out of the dark.

"We're rising high into what looks like the Himalayas," I said to myself as I looked around. Then together with whatever was behind those eyes, I climbed higher.

"There is a cave here," I said and began to laugh at how formulaic it seemed to be taken to a cave in the Himalayas. But whatever was behind those eyes wasn't laughing. It motioned me to follow it into the mouth of the cave and in I went. Shadowy, musty, dank. When my eyes adjusted to the dimness I made out a figure of a sage at the back of the cave. With long white hair and a drooping mustache, he wore white robes and sat in the lotus position. As I walked toward him I heard myself say, "He is a great being," and wondered how I knew this.

But the shaman had told me to ask and so I stood before him and asked, "Are you my helping spirit?" He nodded "Yes," and I was so moved to be in this cave with him that tears came to my eyes. Quickly he took my hand in both of his while I sat before him and although I stared, I couldn't see him clearly enough to make out his features.

I spoke to him anyway, telling him about the coming of the Grandmothers, and that I sought them. "I want to find out why they came to me, I want to know if I can be of service to them." Again he nodded. He knew it all, patted my hand and said, **"It's all right."**

Although his words and tone comforted me I wasn't sure what **"It's all right"** meant, so I asked if it was all right for me to continue on to the Grandmothers. He looked hard at me and then motioned, pointing upward with his index finger.

To reach the Grandmothers I must to go further. Bowing, I offered my thanks and as I rose to my feet I glimpsed an opening in the cave wall just behind his seat. It appeared to lead upward through the cave roof. A passageway. I entered a narrow tunnel and felt my way upward in total darkness.

When at last I reached the mouth of the tunnel and stepped out of the dark into fresh air I was on top of the mountain. But again there was no one present so I must go further still. "Higher," I called out, "I want to find the Grandmothers."

With determination that surprised me over and over again I reached upward, pulling myself higher into a now featureless expanse. In the midst of this upward pull it dawned on me how far the Grandmothers had come to find me. "Did they make this same trip?" I wondered, deeply touched by their effort.

Immediately I began to laugh at myself for thinking in such literal terms. "The Grandmothers," I murmured, "are not ordinary beings." Transparent, wise and all knowing, this journey was no struggle for them.

At last I broke through a membrane-like barrier into an arena where small clouds bounced in the air around me. The light was bright, and it was strangely quiet here. I could tell I had pulled myself to a high place because of the quality of the air. The atmosphere held good feeling; this was a happy land—sunny, misty, soft.

Again I asked for a helping spirit and, if possible, the Grandmothers, and as I waited in the bright mist I heard the laughter of what sounded like young women. I glimpsed vague shapes moving about while with every moment that passed I became aware of the palpable happiness that was this place. The air was thick and sweet, making made me feel expectant–as if I had been brought to the foot of the Big Rock Candy Mountain.

Suddenly the place was charged with holiness and although I couldn't see anyone, I knew that a great being was present. "Are you my helping spirit?" I asked, "Are you one of the Grandmothers?" The being roared with mirth, peals of laughter cascading from its self, one after another. "This," I thought, "is the true sound of good humor and joy."

The mist began to thin while the laughter welcomed me, wrapped and drew me to itself. Now I could see enough to notice a circle of beings surrounding me. I felt them brush against my body and thought, "It's the Council of the Grandmothers, it must be," but I still couldn't see enough to be sure. My heart beat fast in my throat as I waited expectantly, but that bright mist hung over everything, making it impossible to see clearly.

"Whoever these beings are, they are happy together," I said and then noticed one of them sitting off to the side, alone. It was a woman. "Are you my helping spirit?" I asked.

She beckoned me forward and as I approached I saw that she was sitting on a throne. Before I could think about it I bowed before her and blurted out, "I'm so honored that the Grandmothers came to me. It's hard for me to believe, but I am believing it more. I want to know why they came and what it is they want." Finally I became aware of my words stumbling over themselves, and simply asked, "Why did they come?"

A presence wrapped me in love. This was exactly how I had felt when the Grandmothers embraced me on my walk—nurtured, warm and full. "It *is* the Grandmothers!" I cried. "They are with me again." Patting me, full of smiles, these same Grandmothers began to take care of me. This time they covered me, not with a caul, but a robe.

"Grandmothers, thank you for everything you're doing for me," I began, tears choking my throat. I tried to go on but was overcome. "Your message is so beautiful," I struggled to speak, "about women I mean, and the need is so desperate!" Here I broke down completely. "Please," I said as soon as I could speak again, "if I can help you with this work, show me how. How can I be of service? How can I help?"

Quietly and with great dignity they said, **"Let *us* help. Let *us* help you."** They took me in their arms, rocked me like a child, and as I gazed at their kind faces I said, "Yes, yes Grandmothers, any work that is done, it will be you. But is there anything you want *me* to do? How can I implement this message you've given? *Can* I?" I blurted out, suddenly wondering at my own audacity. But, unable to stop talking, I said, "I know you gave me this message for some reason. Do you want me to pass it on?" I was so thrilled to be in their presence again, so overcome with emotion that everything rushed out of my mouth at once.

They stepped to the side to confer privately, glancing over their shoulders to let me know they were thinking over my request. As they carefully surveyed me I became caught in their gaze and locked there, I received the message that they were going to make me one of them. I didn't understand how this was to take place, but I *knew* it.

And before I could consider what this meant, it was good-bye to any lingering attachment to youth and hello to becoming one with the Council of the Grandmothers. There was a bustle of movement; hands touched my hair, arms and back while glowing warmth filled my chest and stomach. I had become larger, warmer, more expanded.

I looked down at myself and saw that the robe with which they had covered me was black and white. These were the colors in their robes too. The mist had gone, and I could now see these wise old women, smiling and waiting for me. A wave of contentment flooded my body as I registered my happiness and theirs.

"You are to come here, sit with us, and be a part of this council," they said. **"This is your rightful place. You are accruing power and stability, and *this*,"** they said, **"is another initiation."**

"The eagle is part of this work," they said, and the memory of the eagle in our garden flashed in my mind. As I glanced at them, understanding dawned. **"The eagle was our messenger,"** they said, confirming my thought, **"he set the action in motion."** Suddenly *they* began to look like bald eagles. Tall and imposing in their black and white robes, these Grandmothers were fierce, almost frightening.

"Grandmothers!" my voice cracked as I stared at them, but forcing myself to go on, I said, "I'm here on earth where I can do some good if you will do it though me. How can I anchor this message for women?" As soon as the words were out of my mouth I felt my eagerness to begin their work building.

Folding arms or wings against their chests they smiled. **"First you need to trust that this *is* your work."** Pausing to let their words sink in, they said, **"This will happen by coming here to be with the council."** Nodding mutely, I watched them, fascinated.

The next thing I knew we were sitting together. High on a formal platform, a dais, we formed a semi-circle and as I sat in silence I became aware of the powerful presence of the eagle. He was with me; he was within me. I felt him, especially in my hands and feet, and as I gripped the edge of the dais, I watched my hands and feet become talons.

With my upper body upright, I took on the towering carriage of an eagle. "Are you my power spirit?" I asked this overwhelming presence inside me. **"Yes!"** I heard the fierce cry.

"This is why I feel such oneness with the great bird," I said, and when I looked at the Grandmothers, they had become eagles too. The council of great eagles sat with fierce expressions and powerful wings. As I watched these Grandmother eagles the phrase, **"Sky mother,"** came to me.

Now my body truly transformed. Fierceness grew; I was taut with muscle, single pointed in focus. I *was* Eagle. I was surprised to note that I was more thrilled than frightened by this power.

"We are bringing to earth something of the sky now," the Grandmothers said, **"doing this in a new way. It is actually an old way, but one absent from earth for a long time."** As they spoke such power built inside and around me that I vibrated with it. **"The earth is going to be infused with this power,"** they said. **"It is being infused with it now."** "I am embodying this power," I said to myself.

The drumbeat changed, stopped a moment and then sped up. This was my signal to return to ordinary reality. "Grandmothers, help me to sustain this power on earth, to sustain it in this body. Thank you," I murmured, hurrying my goodbyes so as not to fall behind the drumbeat. "I'm coming down now."

Turning away from their fierce, black and white forms, I made my way through the layers of the upper world as quickly as possible, arriving in ordinary reality just before the drumbeat stopped. When at last my body stopped quivering I opened my eyes to see the shaman standing over me with tears in her eyes.

My experience left me shaken but filled full. I had been deepened by whatever the Grandmothers did to me on this, my first journey to the upper world. As I thought back over it I mused that though initially their presence wasn't as clear as it had been on my walk along the cliffs, their words and the transmission of feeling were even more powerful than before.

Over time I learned that the Grandmothers appear in different ways at different times. To this day they either show themselves to me as women or as eagles, but sometimes they don't "appear" at all but make their presence felt just the same. I have had many adventures with them, but others have seen, heard or sensed them in still different ways. Since the Grandmothers are aspects of the Divine, they are not limited in form or in method of communicating.

Several years have passed since I first met them and my work with them continues. Simply put, I am their student and they are my teachers. In my heart I am in union with them and I believe this sense of union is what they refer to when they say that I am one *of* them. Yet my place, my role in the cosmic scheme of things is different from theirs.

Whenever it is time for me to learn more from them, I feel them calling to me, almost pulling on me. They pop unexpectedly into my awareness; I may become aware of them as I go about my day. Whenever this happens, I journey to them as quickly as possible.

Often I journey because I have a question about their work. The shaman taught me to state my questions in the clearest language I can muster and this I try to do, speaking my journeys into a tape recorder. When I play back these tapes, I hear the Grandmothers' messages, stated in their words, though since I am I am the one speaking, spoken in my voice. This book is composed of these encounters.

The Grandmothers appeared in September of 1996 and by late November of that year the shaman taught me how to reach them. This process enabled me to work with them whenever I needed to. The journeying method was new to me and because it was unlike anything I had ever experienced, it by-passed the judgments and limits my mind usually places on my experiences. Since I had no idea how to formulate, criticize or evaluate a journey I was forced to let the Grandmothers teach me directly. My mind didn't know how to pigeon hole this one.

Until the Grandmothers appeared, I had lived a pretty "normal" life. Married, with two grown children, I had spent most of my adult life in the same town. For more than twenty years I had maintained a psychotherapy practice, treated individuals, couples and families, taught classes and run workshops.

When I had begun my practice the work had fascinated me and I couldn't learn all I wanted fast enough. Our children were still at home at that time, so I sandwiched my work at a mental health clinic and my private practice in with my responsibilities to my husband and children. It was a full life with a very tight schedule.

I was totally engaged in the work, and knew that the more techniques and approaches to treatment I learned; the more effective I would be as a therapist. So, whenever I could, during evenings and on weekends, I sought more training. I was especially interested in the body/mind connection and found myself drawn to therapeutic techniques that gave the body, mind and spirit ways to work together for healing.

For nearly twenty years I had been fascinated by my work, but recently I hadn't been as enthused about it. There was a nagging dissatisfaction I couldn't put my finger on. Though what I was doing was good work, helping one person at a time no longer seemed enough for me. I wanted more—to be stretched, challenged, utilized to full capacity. I wasn't sure what this "more" I was seeking would look like, but hoped that eventually something would come to me. This was before the Grandmothers appeared.

The Grandmothers turned my world on its head. Following their guidance and going wherever they led was a struggle for me. I was accustomed to having at least some control over my life and felt overwhelmed by the strangeness of these journeys. What was happening to me was simply not rational; I couldn't explain it to myself, let alone anyone else. It was a great adventure all right, but "What," I asked myself, "was I doing?"

It takes me a while to trust things that are not of this world and this stuff was pretty far out. Over the next few years I came to accept the fact that in the midst of the most astonishing experiences with the Grandmothers, I was still capable of wondering if they were real, and if all this was actually happening to me.

Often I listened to my tape-recorded journeys, especially during the first few months when I needed reassurance that I wasn't making up stories or losing touch with reality. As I listened to the tapes and heard the emotion in my voice, the hesitancy in my speech, the pauses, surprises and tears that came up, it convinced me it had all really happened. My years as a therapist had trained me to listen carefully, and now I heard the sincerity in my own voice, the shocking authenticity in my reports. I couldn't doubt their truth.

This work was calling me to a new commitment to trust—trust in the Divine in the form of the Grandmothers and trust in my connection to them. Even though I quickly believed in the Grandmothers, I still had difficulty believing in myself—believing that I, this unremarkable woman, was worthy of receiving what they were giving. As time wore on I learned two important things: to hear truth the way it came to me, not as I had imagined it would show itself, and to trust in my ability to hear it. The Grandmothers were patient with my lack of faith and slowly I learned to follow wherever they led.

Over and over I asked, "Why did they come to me?" until one day I remembered a dream I had had six weeks before they appeared. In the dream a holy man dressed in a long ochre robe who had visited my dreams many times before, came once again. This time he was direct. Walking up to me and looking into my eyes, he asked, **"What do you want?"**

Even in the dream state I was surprised that he would ask this. For years he had worked with me both in meditation and in dreams so he knew exactly what was in my heart. But when in the dream I replied, "Why I want God," he only stared at me, then asked, **"What else do you want besides God?"**

I was dumfounded. What could he mean, "Besides God?" What else was there? I had longed for God all my life. But giving me a knowing look that said, "Think about it," he left and I woke up in turmoil. "What do you want besides God?" became my Zen koan, teasing, frustrating, opening me to a new level of contemplation. The peaceful life I had led before the dream evaporated.

Now and then I had a sense that there *was* something else for me besides God. For a long time I'd had a vague feeling that there was work of some kind for me to do. This made me recognize that with an urge this compelling, I couldn't want just God. I wasn't yet ready to enter the state of bliss.

After the dream I began to ponder and realized that for several years my life had felt slightly empty. I was underutilized and knew I was. I was used to accomplishment and a fast pace. I had raised my children at the same time I taught school and completed graduate school; then I had thrown myself into my practice. Now, after more than twenty years as a psychotherapist, I was no longer finding the work as compelling. Though lately I had branched out further—learned more treatment techniques, had even become a Reiki master, something was still missing.

I had been searching for work that fully challenged me. Now I understood why the holy man had asked his question. He knew I was ready for something more. After I grasped his intention I began to pray for work that stretched me to full capacity.

My mantra became "Give me something to do that uses *all* of me." As I repeated it, the desire to be utilized to capacity grew stronger. The holy man asked what I wanted at the end of July. I began praying for something to do by mid August and in the second week of September the Grandmothers appeared. They were the answer to my prayer.

Another important teaching came to me in November of that year and although it was not directly connected to the Grandmothers, this lesson about truth, honesty and the power of intention became an integral part of my work with them.

Before I met the Grandmothers I had lunch one day with a group of friends and the subject of truth came up. As we talked I realized that although I had always considered myself honest, I wasn't one hundred percent. This bothered me as the desire to be at one with God had taken root in my heart. Now I looked hard at everything in my behavior that seemed to separate me from this goal.

As I listened to my friends I reasoned that to be in harmony with the spirit of God, I needed to behave as I imagined God would. It was time to stop repeating habits I knew were wrong. After we parted, I thought about what I needed to do.

It was time for me to give up any kind of cheating or lying, no matter how harmless it might seem. No more exaggerating stories to look better and no more downplaying my behavior to win an argument with my husband. No cheating.

I decided to simplify my life by cutting falseness out of it. When I caught myself in the middle of embroidering the truth I stopped and responded as honestly as I could, even when it hurt. I held firmly to my resolve—most of the time.

However, the final commitment to truth came at Meinrad's workshop in New Mexico. The way she lives her life and the power in her teaching moved me so that I took my desire for truth one step further. As I stood in her garden, I made a vow to live only in truth. There and then I asked that all falseness be taken away from me. I remember feeling frightened as I did this. It was a big step and I knew it.

After I got home my left front tooth began to ache. This was an old crown that for thirty years had never given me a bit of trouble, but it was throbbing now.

As the ache increased I imagined the worst—what if I needed a root canal? Then, while driving home from an errand one day, I remembered to ask why this tooth was hurting. No sooner had I formed the question than I saw myself in Meinrad's garden, making my vow and asking that all falseness be removed.

I had heard the saying, "Be careful of what you ask for because you might get it," but this was amazing. My request had been taken literally.

As soon as I understood what had happened, I re-worded my vow and the pain was gone in a day. When I made the vow, my intention had related to falseness in my thoughts, words, and actions, but because

I hadn't made myself crystal clear, all falseness was being removed—including the tooth.

This experience graphically taught me about focused intent. It was this sort of intention I would need to work with the Grandmothers.

The Grandmothers are goodness and purity itself. I immediately saw these qualities in them and wanted them for myself. They helped me with this desire by frustrating me each time I came to them with a question not well thought out, an intention less than pure. They simply wouldn't appear unless my desire for their help came from my heart, not my mind. Initially I was so eager, in such a hurry, to contact them that I didn't realize the importance of journeying with a pure intention. I learned quickly.

CHAPTER 3

Beauty/Power is One Concept

"Power is in the Wings"

After the shaman taught me how to journey I was so eager to go again that I gathered my courage the following day, determined to reach the Grandmothers myself. Spreading a blanket on my bedroom floor, I lay down and put on my headphones so I could listen to the tape of the drum. I turned on a second recorder to speak into and, equipment ready, launched myself from the same tree I had climbed the day before. To my delight once again I rose into the sky. But this time I was moving faster.

Before I knew it I had rushed into and through the mountain where I had met the sage, traveling so fast, I didn't even see him. "Take me to the Grandmothers, take me to my helping spirit," I called out as I raced upward, ever upward, exhilarated by my success thus far.

After passing through the same cloud barrier I had encountered the day before, I entered the blank, white land again and peered around for a helping spirit of some kind, any kind. Suddenly, from out of nowhere an eagle stood motionless with wings spread wide in the air.

"Ah, Eagle! Eagle," I cried, "are *you* my helping spirit?" His laughter resounded as his wings fanned the air. The great bird was actually smiling! His wings scooped me onto his back and we were off. Quickly I noticed how thin and cold the air was, we were up so high, but when I wrapped arms and legs around him to keep warm we soared higher yet.

"Oh, Eagle, my helping spirit, take me to the Grandmothers!" I cried with delight, and again laughter was his only response. Thoughts flashed in my mind. "He is one of the Grandmothers. He is one with the Grandmothers." Finally I turned to him, "I don't know how you are related, but take me to the Council of the Grandmothers anyway please." He chuckled at the "please."

As soon as we landed I noticed how he seemed not to walk, but to strut, reflecting his mastery of land as well as sky. I could hardly keep up with him. Hurrying I glanced over and was surprised to see that he and I were the same size. What an enormous bird, nearly six feet tall with a broad chest and a great head. As we walked I watched his wings, noting the patterns of brown, gray and black feathers. He was magnificent.

We passed through an opening into a circle that seemed to glow. A clearing in the midst of a dense forest of pines, it was very white, very light. "What is this place?" I asked, and in the air I heard, **"This is the Council meeting place,"** but there was no one there. Frustrated, I demanded, "Eagle, bring me to the Grandmothers."

Behaving as though he hadn't heard me, he stood quietly at my side. "What is he doing?" I wondered, but when I took another look I discovered that this, the meeting place of the Council of the Grandmothers, was exactly where we were. I hadn't recognized it because the Grandmothers weren't visible but now I became aware of their presence. It was the concentration of light. A potent force filled the space.

Since Eagle appeared prepared to wait patiently, I would too. I might as well sit down. But as soon as my bottom touched ground I felt the power that pervaded this place creeping from the ground into my hips and buttocks. As I sat, filling with power, I became aware of how important it was for me to learn to rest in quiet. "No more straining," I said to myself, "no preconceptions. Only receiving." Closing my eyes, I focused my awareness on the power building within me and sat in silence.

When I looked up, to my surprise Eagle was dancing in the midst of the lighted circle. With him I saw many pairs of wings, folded upward, but moving, dancing just the same. I watched as the wings opened to reveal the Grandmother eagles who formed this circle of light. Quickly I glanced down and saw that I too had wings, wings that seemed to be holding me upright. I was still sitting on the ground, but sitting tall—because of these folded wings.

The eagles danced together. As I watched they began to move into forms I had seen somewhere before. Native Americans made these patterns when they performed the eagle dance. As this thought came to me I felt a slight pull on my heart, a longing to travel again to the Southwest.

Now the drumbeat moved inside me and vibrating into my chest and stomach, it began to infuse the spirit of eagle into me. With each beat, it pounded fearlessness and the regal quality of eagle into my body and mind. With pride I said, "I am eagle."

I looked at the circle again and saw the Grandmothers still dancing with Eagle. But now they moved not as eagles but as women, multi-colored skirts billowing, arms rising and falling in the dance. They were young, these Grandmothers—graceful and lovely. Not young as a child is young but young in their movement, in their spirit.

As I watched I heard myself say, "I want to be empowered," and thought, "I must be, to do this work. I must be empowered if I am to embody the message of the Grandmothers—for women and for earth." When I said, "I want to be empowered," something began to glide through the air, heading toward me. Colors—black, white, brown and gray—eagle colors—were moving in my direction.

Suddenly I was dancing too. My mighty talons stamped the earth and as my wings fanned open, I heard, **"Dancing is a taking on of power."** "I am an eagle dancer," I said. "I am an eagle dancing."

"What must I learn?" I cried to the Grandmothers. "What is it I must take on to anchor your message on earth?" **"Power! Power!"** they chanted. Oh, how my wings were beating.

"Grandmothers I want to take on the power I need. I am willing. Teach me. Show me. Give me the power." I was praying and crying at the same time, but my attention was drawn back to my wings as I felt the pull of their rising and falling.

"It is the wings," the Grandmothers said, **"power is in the wings; movement is in the wings."** It was my wings that fanned and lifted me, expanding my chest and heart. The rising sense of power grew so strong inside that I could hardly bear it. I couldn't contain it. Washed over by wings, my own, Eagle's, and the Grandmothers', and overcome by their rhythm, I dropped into unconsciousness.

When I awakened I asked, "Is there anything more I am to do to become a worthy messenger?" In answer, the Grandmothers showed me myself as a Native American, dancing the eagle dance. Turning to the left with my left shoulder down and to the right, tilting up to the left wing. "Grandmothers," I said, bewildered by all this dancing, "do you want me to do anything but dance?" **"Dance,"** they said, **"dance and listen. Listen to the wind and to the subtle things. Listen to the way things happen."**

After a few moments of silence I cried, "A phallus!" Hardly believing what I was seeing I darted my eyes away, then back again to the Grandmothers who stood dignified in formal posture. In front of them they held a huge, stone penis and scrota. As they lifted this monumental symbol of masculinity, they gazed at me gravely and said, **"The Council of the Grandmothers holds the power of masculine as well as feminine energy."**

I was so shocked I could only stare. "These Grandmothers," I muttered, "are not just sweet, loving old ladies. These are powerful beings." They straightened and tugged on my pinions, especially the big ones at my shoulders and back, strengthening them—and they did this while I was dancing. I had been dancing the whole time. I couldn't seem to stop and I didn't want to. They looked on and I danced until the drumbeat changed, telling me it was time to leave.

> *"Power is beauty*
> *Beauty is power."*

After this journey I realized I must learn the nature of the power the Grandmothers were giving. When they first appeared on the walk above the beach they had spoken of beauty and power although at the time I hadn't understood what they meant.

One morning in December I woke and realized I had been dreaming of the Grandmothers. Quickly I grabbed the notebook from my bedside table and began to write. It was as if I was taking dictation: even though I was awake the Grandmothers were still speaking.

"Beauty/Power is one concept, not two," they said. **"We have come to restore people to full power and beauty, for until they step into their power and honor their individual beauty, the world will be unable to come into balance.**

"Power is beauty.

Beauty is power.

"Power/Beauty is the living out of one's essence. It is not power 'over' or power 'in order to', but being 100% oneself, and living in the truth of who you are. Since beauty is the outward manifestation of one's essence, every being is beautiful when expressing this essence.

"**Beauty/Power is life in action,**" they said; "**truly, it is life manifesting itself.**" I recognized layers of meaning in their words. "If I can grasp this," I said, "I'll have a new way of looking at the world."

"**Judgment by outward appearances, the yang way of looking at the world, is action or product oriented,**" they said. "**This entirely misses the point.**"

"**Living by judgment and measurement of one another, which is how you have been taught to live, goes counter to the expression of the life force within you. This way of living has caused undue suffering; it is destructive rather than life enhancing.**

"**You live in a world where you are judged and in turn judge one another—often harshly. Rarely do you accept one another as you are—according to each one's particular 'essence.'**" They leveled me with their gaze as they said, "**At this time living in a non-judgmental way is beyond your comprehension.**

"**None of you live in a world free of judgment, and women, having been judged for thousands of years to be 'lesser than' or 'one-down,' are accustomed to being devalued. Women have grown accustomed to having all they instinctively know devalued. Women's intuition or inner knowing is dismissed as a joke.**" Shaking their heads and looking rueful, they said, "**You are measured by a masculine yardstick and found wanting. It is to be expected, therefore, that women as well as men see power as 'power over' as this is the only 'power' you have ever known.**"

They were speaking of the difference between yin and yang, referring to the prevailing worldview, one framed by yang energy. The Grandmothers use "yin and yang" to describe the situation that exists on earth today. As Webster defines them yin is "the feminine passive principle in nature that in Chinese cosmology is exhibited in darkness, cold, or wetness and that combines with yang to produce all that comes to be. Yang is the masculine active principal in nature that is exhibited in light, heat or dryness and that combines with yin to produce all that comes to be."

"**We use the terms yin and yang to address a reality larger, more complex and multi-faceted than words can express,**" they said. "**Yin and yang are not perfect descriptions, but they fit best. Individual people and all life on earth suffer from excessive yang and insufficient yin.**"

The devaluation of women and of the Feminine Principle so pervades our world that we have come to expect it. "**Women get furious about the way men undervalue and sometimes debase them,**" the Grandmothers said, "**but how many of you are angered by the way women** devalue other women? Because of the intense push for masculine values, women, as well as men, have become increasingly intolerant of their sisters." We have all come to accept the argument that human beings are created to "produce, compete and win," and those who don't, have no place in the world. Feminine values therefore have no place in it either.

"This yang bias has affected attitudes toward beauty, making beauty itself a commodity to be sought after and acquired. Women instinctively know that beauty and power go together and strive to be beautiful in order to have the power they seek. But beauty without power will always be abused, either by others or by the self. A beautiful woman or man who has no inner power is at the mercy of the world." Beautiful women or men are often preyed upon and in turn prey on the powerful. Beautiful young peoples' lives are often destroyed by too much attention and adulation."

"You seek beauty from without by spending much time and money on hairstyles, clothing, even surgery," they said, "and you seek power from without by striving to accumulate money, influence and fame. It is a pity, as none of these will satisfy you. You will find yourselves always seeking and always disappointed.

"Do not waste time looking outside yourselves for what you think you need. Turn your awareness instead toward the source of power that lies within you. We promise that when you begin to seek inside yourselves, you will find that power and beauty *do* go together.

"When you have the correct relationship to your Self, the higher self, power and beauty blend together and become one and the same, rather like two sides to the same coin. Beauty/Power spring from within and have to do with blooming as the flower that you are rather than from striving to 'do,' or to impress.

"Living in power is the correct way to live. It will not turn you into tyrants who strive to dominate others. No! It will allow you to be more effective in the world and more compassionate with one another. Power is nothing to be afraid of. On the contrary, it is only natural for everyone to embrace the power of the Feminine Principle. It is this embrace that allows you to fully express your nature."

I wrote as fast as I could, and when later I read what they had dictated the depth of their wisdom astounded me.

CHAPTER 4

A Different Realm

"In being in one's place each one is doing something important."

Three days later I journeyed back to learn more. This time, no sooner did I lift from my tree than Eagle flew in, taking my breath away as he picked me up by a harness attached to my waist. From this, helpless but held fast, I dangled. As I bounced in the air beneath him I looked out on the strange new world I was exploring.

The higher we climbed, the more fiercely the wind rushed against me, and as I swung in midair the thought crossed my mind that some of the teaching I was receiving was coming from Eagle and this process of flight. "It's in the flight," I said, deciding to pay closer attention, to feel what Eagle felt as he flew. Suspended from my harness, I tentatively spread my arms, imitating him as he began to circle upward.

My arms became wings and just a dip, a fast climb and I was flying alongside him on my own. With harness gone, I felt the wind blow through my feathers. In mid air Eagle and I stopped and, facing one another, performed a funny little dance step. Then he said, **"I am teaching you about fearlessness. Your mind keeps thinking of falling and these thoughts are getting in the way of learning."**

He was right. Although I had said nothing, on each journey I had battled with the fear of falling. I thought I had done a good job of keeping my fear to myself, trying to overcome it on my own, but Eagle assured me with a pat on the shoulder, **"This is a different realm."** Here he would teach me about fear and *fearlessness*.

The drums were pounding into my consciousness, telling me that I was learning a *new way of being*. Here was a different reality, where I could see things with new eyes.

"Oh my!" I gasped as I suddenly became aware of the amount of fear I had carried in me. Not only fear of flying, fear held within me all my life—I saw it hunkered down inside my body, so huge, it overshadowed me. In terror I held my breath, transfixed by this enormous fear mass now revealed.

Before I could collapse into horror Eagle grabbed me by the harness and off we went, this time breaking through a barrier into space so high, I watched clouds as they drifted below us. We glided along so smoothly, skimming the wind, and though I vaguely recalled that something I hadn't liked just happened, I couldn't concentrate enough to remember what it was. Instead I thought about seeing the Grandmothers again. I wanted to know how I was doing and learn what to do next. But for now I was happy to be flying, swooping along, suspended in the air.

It was clear and cold above the clouds and as I looked around I found that I was alone, a lone eagle, gliding and soaring. "A lone eagle," I thought and heard, **"As is right."**

Colors converged, and then formed rainbow affects that reflected off and filtered through my wings; hues of sunsets and sunrises pooled around me. I watched them shift as they ran through my feathers and someone said, **"The source of all light and beauty is here. This is sun power, the power of God."**

"All of it is on my wings," I marveled, and as I moved forward, I trailed power. "How can such a thing be possible?" I asked, at the same time recognizing how right it felt for this radiance to flow through me. **"This is correct,"** the voice said.

Circling, I climbed higher still; lifting and gliding, it was like dancing in air. Hovering in the thin, cool light where there was nothing to look at or even desire to look at, I rested. As I floated on a current, completely at peace, a voice said, **"Above it all."**

"I am almost at one with the sun," I said and heard, **"The sun is the best friend. The eagle and the sun are best friends,"** and after a pause, **"Theirs is a *real* relationship."** I recognized a deep truth in these words but I was too much a part of what I was experiencing to think about it.

Gliding though the thin air, I drew color behind me—a train of beauty. As my heart swelled with reverence for what I was perceiving, I cried, "Oh teach me, my spirit helper, teach me and make me worthy."

Abruptly Eagle swooped in, turned fiercely to me, and pinning me with his talons and gaze cried,

"REAL INTENT!
LOSE NOT THE FOCUS!
LOSE NOT THE FOCUS!
Have this intenseness," he ordered. **"Do not be distracted."** "Yes, Eagle," I said, swallowing hard while I watched his every move. "Teach me how. Teach me." **"Do not look down,"** he said. I climbed on his

back and as he flew I focused my eyes forward just as he did. When I happened to glance down I saw that there was nothing there.

Swooping suddenly, he began a dive. I saw the familiar white circle approaching, and banking at the last minute, Eagle landed effortlessly in the midst of the Grandmothers. Dismounting and stepping forward I spread my wings for them and gracefully bowed. "Grandmothers, teach me, heal me, make me worthy, ready and able to do the work you have given."

Reaching out their arms, they drew me to themselves, up onto the dais once again where we sat together, very still. As we sat unmoving, it occurred to me that though there seemed to be nothing happening at this moment, by sitting quietly in formation like this, there was something. Observing myself as if from a distance, I saw that I was entirely peaceful, as though I had been meditating for a long time.

"In being in one's place each one is doing something important," they said, breaking the silence. I sensed this "place" they were talking of viscerally, especially in the bottom part of my body. There seemed to be a slot in the dais where I was plugged in, through my talons (my extremities) and through my tail. I was supposed to be in this slot. Being here made everything complete, made everything work. It was good to sit like this. I was like a puzzle piece that had finally found its home.

A memory of eagles at the zoo came into my mind and I thought of how sad it was that these great birds couldn't spread their wings and fly. "How wrong it is to confine them," I muttered, "there is so much of that wrongness on earth." But the place I was in now was different. This place was the *right place*. It called on "rightness," called on things to be what they were, each in its perfect spot, in its perfect way.

No sooner did this thought come than the Grandmothers spoke. **"All creatures aligned with their being,"** they said, **"we are calling that up now, humans included. All are aligning with their being, standing in their proper place. Each one perfect within its nature.**

"What you are feeling is the restoration of the rightness of life." Profound words that sent a vibration thrumming through my body. But before they could say more the drumbeat changed. I cast a questioning look at them, but there was no more time; I had to return to ordinary reality.

"Pain and illness occur where new energy meets the old"

Later that day I returned. Incomplete with the morning's journey, though I was tired, I wanted to go back. "Eagle, come!" I cried as I lifted from my tree.

Almost immediately I saw the mountain before me and was surprised when I didn't go through it. Instead, I quickly rose above it. I hadn't climbed far when something frightening rushed at me—dark and threatening. My heart raced and I felt my hair standing on end. Since I couldn't tell what this darkness was, I did as the shaman had instructed. "Are you my spirit helper?" I cried. Instantly it left.

Relieved that it was gone, now I was really frightened. This thing meant me harm; I knew that with conviction. "Eagle!" I called, and immediately felt his presence. Standing in the air before me, he declared, **"That was a test of fearlessness."**

I was shaking. Why did I need a test like this? I didn't know but I believed him. This thing terrified me so that it got my full attention. If any part of me was unconscious before that encounter, it wasn't now. Patting me on the back to reassure me, Eagle motioned me to follow him.

Gliding beside him felt smooth and easy so I exhaled deeply and let myself relax and enjoy the flight. He began to teach me how to swoop. I loved the sense of grace and power as I whooshed with the wind, gliding and swooping, gliding and swooping. In the midst of my lesson, however, I felt a twinge of anxiety. At the back of my mind lay the thought that I only had so much time per journey, so many drumbeats for each visit to this realm. I wanted to use my time well, to learn everything I could.

At last I interrupted our flight. "I want to be with you, Eagle," I said, "but I also want to be with the Grandmothers. I think I should..." **"RELAX!"** he said and..."Ah h," lifted on an up draft, I was drawn higher yet. I took in a satisfying breath and he said, **"All things happen in their time."** As his words sank in I almost laughed aloud for behaving as if this adventure was my responsibility. "Why am I worrying?" I asked myself. "I'm not in charge of this. It all happens according to the Grandmothers' agenda, not mine."

My awareness of the drumming heightened. Although the drumbeat hadn't changed, there was a shift in vibration, and now I was somewhere else, walking forward toward an opening. "Is this the entrance to the Grandmothers' circle?" I asked. It looked familiar but something about it was not right. "Oh!" I suddenly cried.

Dragons lurked at the sides of the opening. Frightening and monstrous, they menaced me, and tried to block my way. But when I challenged them with, "Are you my spirit helpers?" they departed and I was able to cross beneath the archway of trees and greenery. Once again I was at the white circle of the Grandmothers who sat on the dais, waiting for me.

"Um-m-m..." I crooned, as I noticed that my body had changed and I was now more than my usual self. Within me was an awareness of my humanness and also of my eagle self. I sensed talons, felt the power of my eagle stride and my piercing vision. **"We were interrupted earlier, Daughter,"** the Grandmothers said, **"come forward."** And as I walked toward them, I did so as a person and as an eagle.

I knelt, spread my wings and they drew me to them. With their wings they embraced me and began to work on my shoulders. Touching, adjusting, fussing, they spread my feathers. I stood quietly as they checked everything, adjusting and fluffing, smoothing pinions and feathers. **"Everything in alignment,"** they explained, looking me over.

As they worked I heard them say, **"Eaglet,"** and knew from the word and the way they said it that I was young and in their eyes, magnificent. **"You are doing just right,"** they assured me with loving pats, and I felt a good proud quality inside me, a burgeoning fierceness. This, I realized is how eagle feels. "Thank you," I said, "for my eagle teacher." **"This is your nature,"** they replied.

"Grandmothers, your teaching weighs on me in a wonderful, expectant way and I long to spread my wings and spread your message." Saying this so moved me that I started to cry. They stepped forward as one and placed an amulet around my neck, a token that denoted my job, my purpose with them. There was red and a Prussian blue in this amulet and I as I felt it against my skin I became aware that this deep blue color was all around us too, infusing the atmosphere, permeating the air we breathed. The amulet signified a rank of some kind. Somehow I had achieved a rank. And my wings! Oh, my wings. There was such an expansion and pulling on them!

"We want to see your wings," they said. I arced them open, followed the Grandmothers' eyes and saw that...I had massive white wings now—white at the shoulder at any rate. My wings lifted of their own accord and I began to dance; rather my wings danced me, lifting and dipping me in the air. "A-a-h-h," I cried, almost swooning, as I was propelled forward and backward, up and down by these wings.

"It is time for you to dance like this on earth," they said. In the living room, in the hills behind the house—I must dance. They rubbed unguents into the pinion joints at my shoulders and into my neck where my wings attached to my body. They directed me to take in a deep breath then blow it out, showing me that some of my headaches were caused by my attempts to integrate this increasing power. **"Pain and illness**

occur where new energy meets the old," they said. "The painful places in your body are 'catch points' which occur as a part of change and growth. We will help you."

Encircling me while hovering, they danced round and round with wings outspread. Their wings carried power into mine. Now I turned and faced each Grandmother and danced alone in the midst of their still moving circle. Waves of energy washed over me inside the rhythm of their beating wings. I lifted upward, wheeling and circling above their heads and they charged me with their power.

I circled higher until I could barely see their golden beaks and the darker feathers of their bodies and when I lifted still higher they became specks. In the clear air I felt the cold and hovered for a moment. Then began the graceful downward spiraling, and circling, gliding, circling gliding I returned to the center of the Grandmothers who stood motionless.

Ushering me into their midst, silently they covered me with their wings and I was filled with a great peace, filled with a great blessing. They bent over me and lovingly brushed my head and shoulders, and it felt as if they kissed me with their wings. **"Rest now,"** they said, **"Do no more work for a few days, Eaglet."**

CHAPTER 5

Too Much Doing

I followed the Grandmothers' direction and rested from journeying for a week. These lessons were the most astounding and exhausting I had ever experienced, and two journeys in one day had been too much for me. Although it took me several days to get back to feeling "normal" again, I was so excited about what I was learning from the Grandmothers I couldn't wait to return.

This work was demanding more time and energy than I had thought it would. I was running a tight schedule, sandwiching journeys between clients and between taking care of my home and family. I discovered that I needed a great deal of discipline to refrain from further journeying until I had first transcribed my last adventure with the Grandmothers. I knew it was important to record every bit of their teachings but I was so eager to learn more that I wanted to spend all my time journeying.

When at last my week was over, I prepared to return, and as soon as I lifted from my tree Eagle flew to me. I rose upward in his draft and saw that this time the Grandmothers were positioned directly above the Himalayas, standing in alignment with the highest mountain in the range. "Which one is Everest?" I wondered.

Eagle didn't fly directly to them but landed a short distance away so he could dance up to them *in style*. Exhibiting the most power I had yet seen in him, he was commanding, the aristocrat of the air, and carried his body with heroic grace. I must have been following his lead because I too was confident as I strode forward and stood before the tallest Grandmother, a fierce looking bald eagle with a white head and riveting eyes. Looking into those eyes, I communicated my seriousness; "I am dedicated to this work."

She swept her wings upward and nodded, demonstrating how she wanted me to spread mine. In that movement she said, **"Yes!"** she accepted my dedication.

While I spread my wings she said, **"Three to one. If you want to work with us, you will need more journeys focused on your healing, not only on cosmic truths. Until you are physically strong, you won't be able to retain and use the lessons we are giving you."**

I agreed with her and the Grandmother Eagles smiled knowingly, nodding their heads in sympathy as I confessed to them what a full time "doer" I had always been. How I felt I must do everything myself, took responsibility for whatever was at hand, worried about it and then bossed others around. What a burden and painful habit this had been for me and for everyone. **"We have seen you wear yourself out,"** they said. **"We have watched you teeter on the edge of exhaustion. This comes from an enthusiasm you were born with, plus a habit of over striving. *Too much doing.*"**

From now on I was to journey three times to the lower world for healing for each time I came to the upper world for learning. Gesturing to the area of chronic pain at the back of my neck they said, **"Coming here is hard on the body, thus three to one—three healings to one expansion."**

Several of them leaned forward and with wings expanded, pecked at and straightened my pinfeathers. Fluffing the ruff at my neck, they said, **"Take three healing journeys to the lower world for each expansive journey to the upper world. You need to be stronger and have more power if you are to do our work. We are giving you the power and will continue to do so but unless you do the healing work, the power we give you will have no place to live."**

I must strengthen my body so their wisdom could "live" in me. Since I had already learned from the shaman how to go to the lower world, I was to take my next journey there. We faced one another and nodded our agreement. We had come to an important understanding and as I bid them goodbye I felt happy, ready to return to ordinary reality, with eagerness for the work ahead.

"Feminine power has not been embodied on earth for a long time."

Soon after this the Grandmothers surprised me by showing me my early years, especially my struggle to become a woman. As scenes from childhood flashed before me I saw and felt myself as I was then—not a memory but a re-living. Ten years old, fearful and anxious as I went down the cellar stairs, thirteen, longing for something better to come to me as I swung on the maple tree and gazed down the road.

Reliving the pain and courage of those years gave me so much compassion for my young self. **"When you were growing up you had to teach yourself how to become a strong woman,"** they said. **"The women in your mother's generation and those before her never moved into the power of their womanhood. If young girls have not seen a woman stand firmly and comfortably in her power, the concept of a powerful female will be foreign, even frightening to them. Feminine power has not been embodied on earth for a long, long time."**

When they showed me myself as a young woman I saw how *hard* I had worked at everything, and how *tired* I was. In my attempt to become "powerful," I had juggled graduate school, a teaching job, caring for young children and a husband, and nearly always did two or three things at the same time.

When I saw how I had jokingly referring to this habit as "taking advantage of myself," I cried. Too much striving, too much yang energy and the excessive stress that accompanied it had made me sick. Over time I developed chronic headaches, back pain and exhaustion.

Living for years in endless "doing," I now manifested what they called "the yang imbalance." This was why I must now journey to the lower world. I so desperately longed to live a balanced life, that when they said, **"Your life will become a pleasure as the energy of yin fills you,"** I sobbed in relief.

I had spent my life trying to be all things to everyone, yet all the striving I had done to become "powerful" had made me weaker, not stronger. Over and over again I had tried on the yang model of power only to discover that it didn't fit. So when they said, **"Because of the world's present excess of yang and its insufficiency of yin, woman is suffering from her own impotence,"** I knew exactly what they meant.

"The sun beats down over all, touching everything according to its nature."

True to my habit of "doing," I began my first journey to the lower world, thinking, "If I squeeze my schedule tight enough I can get in one or two journeys to the Grandmothers each week." I wanted to keep on learning—not *waste time* on healing and the lower world. I could see how addicted I was to "doing," but I wasn't yet ready to change my behavior.

However, the Grandmothers had been clear about what I must do; they had said, "Three to one," and although I committed to following their directions I was still convinced I could have it my way. "I'll just journey every day," I said to myself. "That will do it." How out of balance, how full of the energy of yang I was then.

On my first journey to the lower world I found my entrance through a hole in the earth. I had hoped for a more dramatic departure for this level of non-ordinary reality—a cave, a blowhole, something exciting. But when I asked for my entry point, the opening that presented itself looked like a mole hole. As I gazed at it, preparing to jump in, in my mind I heard the word, "sipupu." Months went by before I learned that shamans use this word to refer to an opening to the lower world.

I jumped in and fell head over heels into the darkness of the earth. Rolling and falling, downward I rushed, whistling down a shaft of blackness for what seemed like miles. Now and then I saw pairs of eyes peering out at me from the dark.

At last moving water shone before me, a river, seeming to flow down hill. A canoe rode in the shallows and before I knew it I was inside and paddling down river. The drum beat loud in my ears as I rushed onward, searching for a helping spirit, paddling as fast as I could until I rode up onto a sandy bank.

As I came to the edge of what looked like a jungle the light changed and it wasn't so dark any more. But since no one was at the river's edge, to find a helping spirit I had to move on. I pushed my way through the thick-leaved tropical plants to an opening in the forest.

I looked to my left and before me, towering on his back legs, stood an enormous bear. "Are you my helping spirit?" I asked nervously. I sensed warmth that seemed to come from him and felt a corresponding feeling of fullness in my chest. **"Yes,"** he said. He was my helping spirit, very big, very dark. Taking my hand in his paw he walked me slowly and quietly onward. "I want empowerment and healing," I said as I gazed at his hulking form.

When he remained silent I understood that the work of this journey had begun. Breathing deeply, I looked around, attentive to everything, centering, centering.

We climbed a rocky ledge, my hand in his paw as he led the way. The ledge dropped off into a canyon and we followed a pathway that twisted up the side of the mountain. The path was steep and rocky but I was surprised when I didn't feel the physical strain of it. Although I was aware of its difficulty, the climb didn't tire me. "This is non-ordinary reality," I reminded myself.

The sun was mid-horizon, straight in front and a little to my left. When we reached the summit I sat down on a comfortable-looking rock and gazed at the panorama before us. This was a place of empowerment. I felt it.

Bear stood behind me and rotated his paws in a clockwise motion from the middle of my back on up to the top of my head, around and around to the rhythm of the drum. Whatever he did settled me and gradually I nestled into my seat on the rock and relaxed into the rhythm of the drum. The face of the rock was warm. I drew strength from it, power and solidity, aware that as I sat, its minerals were strengthening me. I was aware of Eagle's presence too; he was perched behind and above Bear and me.

Suddenly I noticed that I was asking the same question over and over again. "Is there something I should be doing, something I should ask for on this journey?" I repeated until at last Bear said, **"Hush!"** I finally did hush, let go of my expectations and gave myself over to the experience. In fact, so fully did I relax that I drifted off, falling asleep until Bear patted me gently on the shoulder. All the while Eagle perched silently, watching with us while peering out over the canyon.

When I finally asked, "What is the meaning of this experience?" I heard, **"Be the rock—steady and unmoved,"** and somehow understood. The rock sees all, from its position looks out over all.

A sharp pain in my side grabbed my attention and as I focused on it, I noticed clouds floating by. **"Passing clouds,"** I heard, **"Passing clouds,"** and remembered that pain is just this—passing clouds. We sat together on the mountain, Eagle, Bear and I, watching the clouds and in a moment the pain was gone while the rock was still warm.

I began to breathe in the energy of the rock. "I am willing to become steady like this rock," I said, recognizing its quality as one I wanted for myself. Then I turned to Bear and asked, "Is there anything else I am to do here?"

The rock turned into a chair—an armchair or throne high up on the mountain and I took my seat on it. Bear stood behind and Eagle perched above while a voice said, **"Master of all you survey."**

For a long time we sat like this—the mountain, the animals and me until Eagle broke the silence, crying, **"Look!"** When I peered into the distance my eyes were drawn to the colored strata layering the walls of the canyon, drawn also to the lush green valleys that folded themselves into the canyon before rolling into the distance. **"There is everything here; dry, arid, fertile—***there is everything here***,"** Eagle and Bear said. My job was to observe all this variety and from where I sat every bit of it was beautiful.

"Oh!" I exclaimed, "This is how Eagle sees; this is why he told me to **"Look."** From the top of the mountain *everything* was just what it *was*, perfect in itself. Eagle is far seeing; he watches the world from a high steady place and at this moment, so too did I.

So grateful for having the perfection of life painted before me, I reverently bowed, especially thanking the mountain and the rock beneath me. And as I gave thanks, I became aware of the mountain's pride in itself. Good, not overweening pride, for the mountain was good in its very being.

In gratitude I gazed at the beauty before me. Bear was with and beside me—supportive in a near and dear way while Eagle was supportive in a dear, more distant way. "This," I said, "is the way they are. This is their nature." **"The sun beats down over all,"** I heard, **"touching everything according to its nature. Not everything requires the same amount of sun, or wants it."**

Turning slowly in a circle with arms upraised, I praised the sun and the four directions, north, south, east and west and as I did this I felt the power of the rock in my feet and in the center of my body. The rock was breathing me in. Moving into harmony with the mountain, I breathed in the rock while the rock breathed me in. "Thank you," I said to Bear, to Eagle, and the mountain as the drumbeat changed.

I was quieter inside myself after this journey. Surprisingly steady in mind and body, I felt no immediate need to return to the lower world.

As I transcribed the tape I had made, levels of meaning I initially missed struck me. I was especially moved when I heard the emotion in my voice as I said, **"The sun beats down over all, touching everything according to its nature."** "Of course Eagle relates differently to me than Bear does," I said. "My relationship with Bear feels personal while that with Eagle feels more impersonal. This is as it should be. I don't need the same kind or amount of energy from everyone." I was getting a lot of mileage out of this quote. As with the journeys to the Grandmothers, each time I re-read this one I discovered something I had missed before. Slowly levels upon levels of meaning within these journeys were revealing themselves.

After several days it dawned on me that if I planned to follow the Grandmothers' "three to one" injunction I had better return to the lower world. I wasn't journeying every day like I had thought I would. I didn't feel that compulsion. Perhaps my old habit of striving was changing.

"The great Mother…is patient and waits."

As I dived through my opening into the darkness of the lower world I called out, "Bear, come now. Take me to a place of healing." No sooner did I beach my canoe and break through the leaves of the jungle than there he was, roaring, up on his hind legs, his mouth wide. He was enormous and the red of his gaping mouth terrified me! But I remembered the shaman saying, "A roar from an animal spirit is a greeting, not an attack," so I took a deep breath and made my request. "Please give me clarity of mind, strength of body and purity of heart so I can do the Grandmothers' work," I said, my heart hammering in my chest. "Well spoken," he replied, with a curt nod.

Facing one another, with folded hands/folded paws we bowed, then walked arm in arm to the measured cadence of the drum. Like an old-fashioned couple, we walked abreast up a narrow path and as we turned a corner I noticed that today we were climbing a different mountain. This one overlooked a soft, green valley, with moss-covered rocks, like Ireland.

We began to scale this mountain, and now seriously climbing, upward we went. Bear was on all fours and so was I; it was a handhold here and a foothold there in an increasingly barren landscape as we hauled ourselves upward.

We reached a plateau and there, beside a pathway was a window-like hole in a boulder. The opening didn't seem large enough but Bear went through it easily and so I followed him down a passageway inside this dark hole. I was a little unnerved by the utter blackness, but though I couldn't see him ahead of me, I could feel him, and touching the sides of the cave helped me orient myself. The walls were cool and dry while the cave's floor was covered with fur.

This was his lair; his 'looks within' place. He patted me to welcome me, and at the same time pushed my shoulder down so I could scoot in. Nestling into his cave I made myself comfortable.

I lay on my back, looking up, and through a hole in his ceiling watched the stars. It must have been nighttime because the sky was full of them. As I watched I snuggled up to Bear, thinking "Until now this cave has been only for him but now, thanks to him, it's for me too. This is a special place, where you can go to be alone in a wonderful way—without being lonely."

As he relaxed beside me, I could tell that Bear had come here many times and was completely at peace with being alone. Nodding "Yes," he laid a paw on my forehead, encouraging me to close my eyes, which I did. With him beside me, I was safe and comfortable.

With eyes closed it was the drum alone that carried the journey forward. **"The seasons come and go,"** it said. **"The world outside changes but this place remains the same. This cave is a good place to be; all the worries in your mind have no home here."** This place is eternal, I realized, an inner sanctum and from somewhere in my body came the understanding that it held yin, the recessive quality of woman.

The drumbeat softened and now a female voice spoke. **"The Great Mother is full of life,"** she said. **"She is patient and waits, because life grows naturally."** "It's Gaia who is speaking," I said; "it's all women She is talking about.

"All around me is brown and green; I am covered by the richness of the earth." Gradually I became aware of a sense of expansion and an increasing depth, breadth and volume inside myself. "I am *sinking into HER!*" I cried, "sinking into Mother Earth—becoming massive!

"I'm seeing and feeling differently than I ever have before," I said in wonder. "I'm so much bigger! Mother Earth is one with all souls. She is one with the consciousness of all animals. They are here!" I cried, "They are in this cave." I was sobbing now, overcome by emotion.

When I looked back at the roof of the cave, I no longer saw stars, but animals. Covering the roof were drawings of animals; interconnecting, they merged and blended one with another. "Here," I said, "is a mammoth and a woman, drawn so that they are almost the same form. And this rabbit is connected to this horse." Drawings overlapped so cleverly that I couldn't be sure where one ended and another began. Each figure was part of the next. The artist had shown life merging with and emerging, one form from another.

Tears streamed down my cheeks as I watched, and with each moment that passed I became even larger. I grew deeper and more expanded until finally I heard myself cry, "I am one with HER!" I had merged with Mother Earth.

"Oh, Bear," I wept into his furry shoulder, "Thank you for bringing me here." By now my head was so swollen with tears that pain pounded my left temple. Patting me gently as he rocked me in his huge arms, he murmured, "Sleep."

I was so drowsy and my head hurt so badly that I couldn't keep my eyes open and though I wanted to lie down, I was worried. How would I find my way out of this cave if the drum signaled me back? What if I didn't return to ordinary reality in time? Bear patted me, growled and made little grunting noises as he chuckled at my linear mind.

I looked up at his trustworthy face and realized that this *was* pretty funny. After all, he was my helping spirit; it was *he* who brought me here. And besides, I was now one with Her, one with Mother Earth. This was my last thought before I dropped into a welcome sleep.

In a few moments I was awakened by a message. Softly Gaia spoke, **"I rejoice in all the animals,"** she said. When I opened my eyes, I saw light shimmering in the drawings on the cave roof. "These animals are sacred—part of the Great Mother," I said as understanding dawned. "Oh," I said, as it came to me that the caged and farm produce animals in our world are not fully real. They are not fully themselves, not what they were originally designed to be. They have become homogenized, formed according to human, not divine plan. It is the wild animals that are real. Enormous waves of love for them washed me as I became aware of how *much* I loved them.

"I am *them* and they are me," I said.

I was now so at one with life that there was no fear of any kind left in me. Joy flooded my body. I was *alive*; not only at one with *my* form, I was at one with *all* forms of life.

This sense of oneness awakened in me instantly, with utter clarity. I had never seen anything glow as brightly as the life depicted on the roof of this cave. I had never loved anything more. "Thank you, Bear," I said to my ever near, increasingly dear companion as the drumbeat changed. I turned to go, and leading me by the hand Bear showed me the way.

The Grandmothers and the spirits of the lower world continued to surprise me by their unorthodox teachings. The painting on the roof of Bear's cave was something I would never forget. I now had a picture, a prototype of "we are all one" in my head.

Rarely did the Grandmothers explain an idea to me and let it go with that; working with them always meant expecting the unexpected. They and the animal spirits seldom used the lecture method but involved me in their lesson before I knew what was happening. And each time this element of surprise circumvented my defenses and launched their teachings straight to my heart.

I have never taken a journey knowing what to expect, but because the lessons that come are so original, I always know it is not my mind making up stories. I could never come up with the things they do. **"We give lessons the way we do to create a shift in your perspective, to break up stuck patterns of thought,"** the Grandmothers say.

"Nothing takes place only in a dream or only in the physical world or only on the mental plane."

The Grandmothers were right about my need to journey to the lower world. My headaches were lifting and my backaches easing. Once I realized the benefits of working with the helping animal spirits I stayed with their three to one formula for many months. In the end what surprised me most about these "healing" journeys was how much I learned from them. Each day I marked my notes according to whether the journey was for healing or for teaching, but when I went back over these notes, I saw that some of the greatest teaching came to me on the healing journeys.

Often the helping spirits took me to a canyon deep within the earth where they covered me with a reddish-colored mud, saying, **"fall back now, be cared for. No work."** Their words sounded just like the Grandmothers.

That mud was comforting and I would relax in it as I would at a spa. I might begin a journey with a sick headache and when I returned the headache was gone. "How could this happen?" I asked myself, "How can a journey to non-ordinary reality affect me in ordinary reality?"

One day the Grandmothers addressed this question. I had just arrived and was standing before them when I felt a sharp pain in my heart that seemed to arbitrarily come and go. It was similar to heartburn, but because it was occurring in the upper world I knew it had to be more. Reading my mind, they said, **"You are correct. The pain you are feeling is not only physical."** Patting me reassuringly, they said, **"Nothing is only one-dimensional. Nothing takes place only in a dream or only in the physical world or only on the mental plane."**

Even in ordinary life I had noticed how the universe never wastes opportunity. Whenever one area of my life changed, change rearranged other parts of my life too. As I stood before the Grandmothers with that stabbing sensation in my heart, I knew that a painful change was taking place on some level. Maybe it was physical; maybe it was emotional, spiritual, or all of them at the same time.

The Grandmothers often paired their teachings in non-ordinary reality with something I would hear and see in daily life. These seeming "coincidences" shocked me at first, but as time went on I learned this was one way they were building my trust in them and their teachings.

Even travel was taking on new sense of adventure, as I never knew what I would stumble upon that would corroborate one of their lessons. The helping spirits of the lower world had used red healing mud during my journeys, so I associated it with the realm of non-ordinary reality. That was before I went to Chimayo.

The January following the Grandmothers' appearance, my husband and I drove to a shrine, the Sanctuario of Chimayo, New Mexico. We arrived as mass was being conducted so we slipped into the small room at the side of the sanctuary, a room crowded with people, bent over and digging with spoons through a hole in the church floor. I kneeled to see what they were spooning up. What they had come for was red earth. I hadn't known that pilgrims travel from the corners of the earth for this red healing earth but as I stood back and watched them dig, the Grandmothers' words sounded in my mind: **"Red earth is sacred to the Mother."**

In April of 1998 a friend and I took a trip through the countryside of France. In the Dordogne region we drove to the prehistoric cave of Peche Merle that had been discovered by some local boys in the 1920's.

To step into the cold darkness of this underground world was to step back in time. When the guide shone his flashlight on the walls, paintings of running horses came alive. Handprints from those who once used this great labyrinth marked other walls and in one chamber a human footprint had hardened from the mud of a million years ago.

We were almost at the end of our tour when the guide directed us to a small cavern and with his flashlight illuminated a drawing on the roof. Executed millions of years ago, the drawing seemed at first no more than a jumble of lines and shapes. Amid the many crossing, crowded lines I saw bulls, deer, buffalo, horses, a rabbit, and a woolly mammoth.

As he pointed to a section of the drawing he said that some thought this was a woolly mammoth and some said it was a woman with long hair. He was speaking French, so I have no idea how I understood him but when he flashed his light on this drawing I began to shake. As I stared at the longhaired mammoth/woman I recognized the figure I had seen over a year before inside the cave with Bear.

Once again forms were merging with forms. Animals, plants and humans had been drawn in one grand design just as they had been in the cave of my journey with Bear.

One year later and many thousands of miles from home, I again felt the reverential merging, life's underlying unity as the visionary world and the material world showed themselves as one and the same. As I stood in the cave, tears streamed down my face and the Grandmothers spoke. "All the experiences you have had with us in the past and all that you will have with us in the future are real. Haven't we told you? We are not limited, nor really are you. Different forms of reality can overlap, can sometimes become one and the same."

CHAPTER 6

We Fill You Full

"This was exactly what you needed to get beyond the fear of exposing yourself."

At this point I had only told two spiritual friends about the Grandmothers. I was determined not to speak to my colleagues about my experiences. If I were to let this information slip I would lose credibility as a therapist. After all, who would refer clients to someone who "journeyed to the Grandmothers?"

It had even been difficult to talk to my husband about what I was going through, though I had shared some of the Grandmothers' information with him. Not too much though—I didn't want to scare him.

What I was learning was precious to me, plus I was unsure of myself. All I could do was now and then drop a bit of a journey into my conversation with Roger, like salt sprinkled into soup. I might say something about the changes taking place in the relationship between yin and yang, then hold my breath and wait for a response. But although he was happy to see me excited about this work he didn't understand what I was talking about.

I sympathized with him. As I struggled to communicate what I was learning, my explanations of the imbalance between yin and yang and the power of the Feminine Principle were not clear. It was difficult for me to grasp, let alone explain. There was a chasm between what I was beginning to understand and what I could communicate. My children were only mildly interested in the Grandmothers and I wasn't sure if my old friends would be either. I was in a lonely place.

I was living a private life, and often felt overwhelmed by it. At times I would ask myself, "What am I doing? Is this stuff even real?" It was hard to believe that things had happened the way they had—that the Grandmothers had appeared on the walk at the beach, the eagle had perched on the stepladder in the back garden, and now I journeyed regularly to the upper and lower worlds. It sounded bizarre even to me, and some days when I could glimpse the humor in it I might laugh until I cried.

To ground myself in reality I re-read what I had written the first time the Grandmothers appeared. Each time I read what was on that page I realized with fresh clarity that those ideas were not mine. That helped.

Patient with my lack of faith, the Grandmothers got me to laugh at my need to formulate everything. **"We know how hard it is for humans to have faith in anything that is not of the material world,"** they said. **"In this you are no exception."** They would gently poke fun at my disbelief, rolling their eyes as if to say, **"Again?"** whenever I took a dive into doubt and despair.

But soon after the trip to Chimayo even though I was still afraid of the reaction I might receive, I began to feel an urge to share their message. Where this shift in attitude came from I do not know. Perhaps I was simply tired of holding everything inside myself. At any rate, since I wasn't sure how to come out with their message, I began to pray for the eagle's courage and intensity of purpose, plus the right people to share it with. Soon my prayer was answered, though not in the way I had in mind.

My opportunity came in the form of a lunch meeting when my friend Carol invited me to join some women who had formed a spiritual support group. At least that's what I thought she said.

Carol knew a little bit about the Grandmothers and wanted to know more. Since she had invited me to join this group I assumed these women were also interested. This was the opportunity I had been praying for and now that it had shown itself I was eager to share about the Grandmothers. At last I would get support for this work.

As I write these words I see how far removed from courage I was then. I was actually waiting for support to come to me from others. Luckily the Grandmothers knew just what I needed even though I didn't.

It was a beautiful day and as we gathered around the picnic table, everyone seemed thoughtful and interesting. We were to eat lunch, and one at a time, share our experiences. One woman went before me and though her story of her recent experiences didn't sound particularly spiritual to me, when it came my turn to share, I launched into a description of my encounter with the Grandmothers.

As the women listened I watched their expressions change. I thought they looked a little strained but reasoned this was probably because they needed a clearer explanation. So I tried harder.

I was going into more detail when one of them announced she had heard enough. Then she began to *yell* at me. Who did I think I was? And what in the world was I talking about?

The wave of fear that arose as she berated me was HUGE. I literally quaked in my seat, gripping the edge of the picnic table with my fingernails. What had gone wrong? I looked across the table as her face got redder and redder, thinking I had certainly picked the wrong group to share *this* with.

Later the Grandmothers let me know this had not been the wrong group, nor had it been a bad experience. **"Far from it,"** they happily assured me, **"This was exactly what you needed to get beyond the fear of exposing yourself."**

My prayers had been answered. What I feared most happened to me. I exposed myself, *was* rejected and ridiculed. I never saw any of these women again but months later, when Carol and I were laughing about what had happened that day she told me that one woman had later confided her worry about me—I had obviously been seeing "apparitions." Carol said I had misunderstood the purpose of the lunch group. It was not a spiritual group at all, just a place for women to get together and talk.

When I realized my false expectations I laughed so hard that tears poured down my cheeks. The Grandmothers had played with me and taught me well, led me down the path to where I needed to be.

"All that is necessary for a woman to receive our empowerment and a man to receive the cloak of comfort is a sincere heart and the desire to receive what we have to give."

When I next journeyed to the Grandmothers, I said, "I want to talk to you, Grandmothers. When I do your work I want to be impeccable: I want to do it absolutely right." I confessed my fear of being criticized, and heads tilted, they smiled understandingly and said, **"We know this.**

"Believe in Self. Capital S!" they emphasized. **"Whenever you communicate with human beings you must remember that humans do not live in the land of Self, but in the land of the small self. It is hard for them to take in the message of the Self, so do not listen to them. Keep your eye on your goal."**

"Grandmothers," I said, "I'm so glad to be with you. There is no one who understands all this on earth. No one I can talk to, and I need my own kind." **"We know,"** they said, taking my hands in theirs.

When they released my hands, my arms lifted and became wings, wings covered with rich, full feathers. Seeing these feathers reminded me of how strange life had become for me, how out of place I now felt in my everyday life. Suddenly I remembered the feeling of the lone eagle in flight, the power and rightness of Eagle's way of being. **"The eagle is not a gregarious creature,"** the Grandmothers said. "I understand, I replied, "and I accept.

"How do you want me to pass on your empowerment?" I asked, and they said, **"Call together good, spiritual people who are wanting more. Do this at your home."**

The ceremony of empowerment was to take place in the shady part of my back garden. I would have liked to do it where the eagle had landed but there was more privacy under the fern trees. **"The shady place under the pepper and fern trees will be fine,"** they said, and added **"fire."** Immediately I saw a flame. I would include a candle in the ceremony. **"Go outside for the ceremony,"** they said. **"The spirits of the trees will help to hold a sacred space.**

"All that is necessary to receive our empowerment is a sincere heart and the desire to receive what we have to give. But although no ceremony is necessary, ceremony helps you recognize what you have received.

"Ceremony stops the incessant chatter of the mind. That is why receiving our empowerment in a ceremonial way allows the gift of the caul to go deeper into the psyche and the body." Checking to be sure I understood, they said, **"To have its maximum effect, the experience needs to be visceral and emotional as well as mental.**

"Make an altar by the pepper tree," they said. **"Gather there and call on all forms of the Divine. Have each one stand to receive the caul or cloak of comfort; let them feel their feet on the earth. As they step toward the fire, they can ground themselves through their feet, and then receive. After this the group can surround them."** Explaining, **"As we embrace them, you also embrace them,"** they said, **"begin now to establish this sacred area.**

"Before the ceremony, speak and explain things. *We* will speak," they said. They would speak through me. **"Do not worry about this,"** they said. **"Simply share what happened to you, share the truth of the great yin, *the separation of woman from her essence, of man from his source of support* and what this has done to the world. Tell them how man suffers from his own tyranny and depravation, how woman suffers from her impotence."**

Note: When they spoke this last sentence, the word I heard them say regarding men was "depravation," although many months later, I learned that they said, and meant, deprivation for men are deprived of the softness, the nurturance of yin.

Drawing themselves up, regal, magnificent, they announced, "*Now is the time for the return of the Great Mother of the world. The world needs mothering now.*" After a moment of silence they continued, "**Let each one open to the Great Mothering and then be silent.**" The period of silence would allow this gift to sink deeper into her and his heart.

"**There is a latent spark within each being, and it is this spark that our initiation ignites. The spark turns to flame as each one's essence, which had until that moment lain dormant within them, ignites. This is the purpose of our empowerment.**

"**After receiving the empowerment, each will begin to bloom in her and his own way. They will bloom as the flower that they are and have always been. And since no two flowers are the same, even the color of the caul or cloak of comfort they receive will be different from that of every other.**"

Reading my anxiety about how much responsibility I had in this work, they said, "**Your work is easy. All you need to do is pass the spark from us to them.**" Smiling broadly, they said, "**Do the work joyfully, as an igniter of the spark.**" Squeezing my hands, they whispered, "**Have no fear. The work you do is good, and as you trust in it and in us, it will give you joy. This joy will infuse your life.**

"**We will always give you whatever power you need in order to do this work—no more,**" they said. "**Too much would blast and offend others, and too much power would not be good for you. But don't worry. You will have what you need. The power we give is incremental and will always suit the work you do.**"

"Please guide me to do this right," I said. Running their eyes over me, they said, "**When you have a strong feeling, when you feel something emotionally as well as in your body, follow it. If it is of the mind only,**" they paused and raised a finger, "**know it is not a true feeling.**

"**If you feel an aversion to someone, trust that. Something is not right.**" Explaining, "**The *physical and emotional feelings are not of the ego*; mental thought battles and disagreements with self are.**"

I sent out invitations for the empowerment, to take place on the 22nd of January, and because I didn't yet understand about the Grandmothers' gift for men, I sent these only to women. Several years would pass before men began to attend the Grandmothers' meetings.

When the day of the empowerment dawned I began to wonder if there was anything else the Grandmothers wanted me to do or say, anything I hadn't already thought of? I could hardly control my nervousness and so two hours before the women were to arrive, I put on my headphones and journeyed.

Eagle flew to me as I lifted from my tree and positioning his wings beneath me, protected and supported me all the way to the Grandmothers. As I flexed my pinions and bowed before them I felt greater power in my wings and when I tilted my head and looked down, I saw that they were darker now, just underneath the tips.

Standing before them, my mouth dry with excitement, I said, "Grandmothers, today is the day I pass on your empowerment. Is there anything more you want me to know?"

"The place under the fern trees that you have been working to make sacred will be aligned with this circle today," they said. This was something I was to remember, especially at the moment of empowerment. They showed me the relationship between the fern trees in my garden and their circle in the upper world, and I sensed a line up, a pull of one to the other. Aligned with the gathering spot in the garden, the Grandmothers' circle hovered directly above it. **"Remember this,"** they said.

I was fascinated by this idea of interlocking realities but again my wings drew my attention. Not only were they darker and more powerful, they were wider, more far-reaching than before. As I observed these changes, my wings began to perform a dance of their own, first one, and then the other one curved in, and lifted up. My wings rose and fell with humor and began to move me. I laughed as I lifted up and dipped down, dancing with my wings while the Grandmothers watched, clapping in delight.

There was so much joy! As I looked around, the very air shimmered with it. Beaming, the Grandmothers seemed to broadcast love to me. **"You never thought you would have this joy, did you?"** they asked.

I was speechless, filled with happiness. But there was more. A sensation of fullness and effervescence bubbled up inside me and I gasped, "*This* is the presence of God!" And when I looked down I knew that *God was in my wings.* They were now overlaid, duplicated many times over by ever-greater wings. Concentric transparencies of numinous color beat up and down, and overlapping, my wings stretched into infinity.

Pinks, golds, yellows, oranges, blues, all of these and more flashed from my beating wings until the entire sky took on these colors. I heard, **"Cover the world,"** as the wings beat on, pulling joy into my body, into my body and over the world.

I was in tears—the beauty so great it overwhelmed me. "Grandmothers," I sobbed, "I have nothing more to ask." Silently we embraced and as I flew out of their valley Eagle went with me. **"Goodbye, fledgling,"** he called.

Eleven women came to the garden that day. I had invited thirty, but eleven walked through the door, eleven unusually beautiful women—beautiful in their love of God and of humanity. Including me, there were twelve of us. "Twelve women," I penciled into my notes, "and twelve in the Council of the Grandmothers—an auspicious beginning."

The Grandmothers were present during the ceremony just as they had promised, and every woman felt them. As I explained their message part of me stood back and marveled; it *was* the Grandmothers speaking. Their words flowed from my mouth to the heart of each woman and their love poured through me in endless supply. It was a humbling feeling to be part of something so holy.

When the ceremony was over I wondered how well I had explained the Grandmothers, but at least what I had said hadn't shocked or offended anyone. Yet, magnificent as the empowerment was, I was glad when it was over. While everyone was present I was filled with endless energy but as soon as the last woman went out the door I went to bed.

"Belief in Self is primary. We believe in you."

The way the Grandmothers worked during the gathering was astounding; so much power surged through me that I was high—plugged into the Source. But my body couldn't sustain their energy and I crashed. Too tired to do much of anything afterwards, I just wanted to rest. It took me a full week to integrate the experience and be ready to work again.

When I finally began my next flight to the upper world, I followed in Eagle's wake. We hadn't gone far, however, when I noticed that I was struggling to keep up with him. "Why is this?" I wondered.

Eagle saw me lagging and took me on his back. **"Just enjoy the flight,"** he said. I took him at his word, lay down on his back for a few minutes and when I felt strong enough, he let me try again to fly on my own, spreading his wings below me, just in case.

"You have been away too long," the Grandmothers said as they lifted me onto the dais. From this I understood that when I was tired, they wanted me to come to them, and not retreat into myself.

As they gathered close I saw that some of them wore dresses while some were in their eagle selves. "I'm happy to be with them, however they are," I said and before I knew it they had formed a circle around me. With arms upraised, they stepped in toward me, and as their arms/wings swooped down, they danced away. They danced an in and out motion that seemed to pull fatigue out of me while infusing strength in. In and out, in and out—I felt this rather than understood it.

Waves of power rushed in as they circled. I was being filled. They were caring for my wings too—brushing, fluffing and straightening my feathers.

"You must be with your own kind," they said. **"You must come to us more often."** Gazing at me intently, they said, **"Do not try to do this alone; come to us. All will happen in *our* time. There is no hurry."** As I turned to them, twelve pairs of eyes focused on me. **"Belief in Self is primary. We believe in you. Turn to us and we will help you learn to believe in yourself."** Coming to them was not only for learning as I had previously thought. Like the spirits of the lower world, they too would help with healing—a different type of healing.

Turning in a circle we stepped together in a clockwise direction. When I interrupted the dance to ask for information for further empowerments they cried, **"Receive! We do not teach you on empty. We do not give when you are not fully present. *You have forgotten that you are one of us.* This must be restored first."**

As they tightened their circle and danced closer, of its own accord my spine straightened. The intense expressions on their faces let me know that what they were about to do was important.

Suddenly I was solid. My feet were anchored to earth, my body was straight and strong, I was in alignment with *them.* I watched power shoot up from the earth as they fused me with themselves and with the earth—this so I wouldn't float off, get lost in space and forget who I was. **"For you to do this work,"** they said, **"fusion with us and with earth is necessary. This will anchor but not restrict you so you can still move into other realms."**

I was compact, grounded, and yet not confined. In fact, although my body felt anchored to earth, I watched myself as I floated in the air, so far above ground that I could see into the distance for what seemed forever. Merged with the Grandmothers as I was, I saw everything. Far seeing, I was far-knowing as well as grounded—all at the same time.

Expanding into oneness with the earth involved expanding into other dimensions as well; I was anchored to Mother Earth and at the same time expanded into the galaxy. And it was all happening *now*. When I turned to them for confirmation they said only, **"Receive."** I was fully present in the moment. Usually some part of me spaced out or held back. Now I was *present*.

The Grandmothers were removing blockages. I watched as they reached in and pulled old attitudes and perceptions out of my mind and psyche. That in and out movement worked like a magnet, suctioning fatigue and psychic garbage out.

As they danced, flickers of memory, sensations of pain and heat rose into my awareness and then subsided or were supplanted by sensations of peacefulness and relief. "Take it all, please," I said, "take all the holding back. Take it all."

"We fill you full. Let us."

After a journey to the lower world, I returned to them again. This time I wanted to know how to be more grounded, effective and confident in Self. I launched from my tree, declaring this as my intention, and as I broke through the cloud membrane into the first level of the upper world Eagle sailed in on my left, looked at me with his funny, fierce face and said, **"I can't help you with the grounding part."**

Side by side we flew upward and when I saw the Grandmothers' white circle he taught me how to swoop into it. It was much easier this time; swooping in was like skiing air. I walked toward them my heart sang, "Glad, glad, glad to be here."

Standing in formation, their wingspan covered the earth, wrapped and held it from underneath. **"This,"** they said, **"is the power of the above nurturing and holding the below. What you see is similar to the way Mother Earth holds the earth from within."** As they spoke I thought of the Hermetic Principal, "As above, so below; as below, so above." Was this the same idea? **"Yes,"** they nodded.

"Grandmothers," I said, "It's hard for me to feel peaceful, and as if I belong on earth now. I have difficulty grounding myself." They laughed and replied, **"As if there is only one place you belong!"**

"I am having a hard time living a normal life," I said, trying again to make myself clear. "Since you came that morning in September, I haven't felt like I belong on earth. I don't know how to relate to daily life." I waited, hoping for a response but they said nothing, didn't even look at me. So my attention wandered from their faces, turning inward to myself.

From off in the distance I observed myself and watched this "me" walk forward in deep snow. I was clad in my eagle body, and as I took a step forward, I became fascinated by my great bird feet. Complete with talons, they were the size and shape of snowshoes. At each step a huge foot sank through the snow, then plunged through the layers of the earth's strata. Although my feet penetrated the earth, my head remained high in the clouds. I was above, I was below, I was in all worlds at the same time.

"Nothing is one dimensional," sounded in my ears and as I took another step I watched my talloned foot sink into and through the earth. Down, down it went. **"Each step is no longer on the surface,"** the Grandmothers said. **"Now there is deep contact."**

"Think of who you ARE!" they cried, and holding me with their eyes, said, **"Think of the greatness of your being, not of your little self, but of your great Self, that which is one with the source of all."** I concentrated on their words, asking them to give me an experience of this Self and in less than a second I swelled and swelled.

Although I was still aware of being inside my body, whatever "I" was, was so much bigger, so much more than this body, that it was making me dizzy. "Grandmothers," I called, "Help!"

Shooting me a stern look, they said, **"You need to go to the lower world more often—to heal, ground and orient yourself. This is the only way you can do this work."**

This expansion was almost more than I could bear. I felt faint and began to berate myself for becoming sloppy with their three to one formula. I'd started taking breaks from journeying, turning away from non-ordinary reality whenever I felt overloaded. Then when I resumed, instead of going to the lower world for healing, I'd gone back to the Grandmothers for more information. I'd been cheating, and couldn't get away with that any more. The energy they had just given me was more than I could hold.

"All right, Grandmothers, I will be impeccable in following your orders. But as long as I'm here could I ask some questions about your work? About our work," I quickly corrected myself. **"Good!"** they said, and folding their wings against their chests, they looked me over, amused by my tenacity.

"Should I write a book about this?" I asked. **"We will write the book,"** they said. **"This is the work you will do,"** they said, affirming our work together. **"Do it. Let bud follow flower, let twig follow branch. We will guide you. Keep faith and do it."**

"Are there any lessons to accentuate the teachings you have given me?" I asked. "Anything others need to hear?" I had asked this on an earlier journey but it came out of my mouth again.

They were silent and so I too remained silent and as I turned within myself I was amazed to find the presence of the Mother nestled inside me. Her love flowed throughout my body; *She* was living inside *me*. And because She was there, I recognized myself as part of something enormous and magnificent.

Love flooded in, then out from me, but I was in no way depleted by this outpouring. Because the love wasn't mine, it was Hers, all Hers. There was no separation between what was Her and what was me. As love filled my body, then poured out from it the Grandmothers spoke. **"Diminishment of self occurs when you think that you, the little you, are depleted or made less by giving."** Smiling a secret smile, they said, **"In truth this is not so.**

"First fill," they said. **"Allow the filling of the little self with the big Self. This must be first. Take time for this. Let filling be first and let it be complete. Then your giving will be effortless, unconscious. There will be no karma attached to this sort of giving, no anything attached to it. This sort of giving,"** they smiled, **"is as easy as breath."**

Before me appeared a lovely room. Morning light flooded through a small paned window onto a table set for breakfast. On the table sat an over-sized pitcher, broad and sturdy, with a generous mouth and gracefully curved sides. The color of cream, as sunlight poured over it the pitcher gave off a glow and a sense of abundance. The golden light pouring through the window made everything in the room seem to be filled with and made up of light.

When I took a closer look I saw that the pitcher was filled with more than light. Not only the color of cream, it was *filled* with cream. Cream, thick and heavy, bubbled right up to the top. A pottery cup sat next to the pitcher and streams of light rained over it too.

As the Grandmothers poured from the pitcher into the cup the pitcher magically refilled. Perhaps it was the sunlight that kept it full, but no matter how many times they poured, cream still rose up to the brim.

"Think of this cup and pitcher. We fill you full. Let us," they joyfully said, cupping their palms to show how we are to receive. **"By**

thinking of us and of the Net of Light of which you are a part, we will fill you and keep you ever filled."

They had shown me the Pitcher and Cup, but what was this Net of Light they had mentioned? They wouldn't say, but instead cried, **"No more emptiness! And from *this* state of fullness, the act of giving takes place. So easily you won't even think of it as giving, so easily there will be no separation between giver and receiver. The giving will be all one."** Beaming joy, they added, **"Part of the flow from the source of which you are a part.**

"Filling full abolishes all sense of separation from the source, abolishes all sense of smallness, need, or of being less than. That is gone," they said. **"There is only Being Full, and from that state everything flows easily.**

"Enjoy this," they said, **"and your life will become easier and easier—as it should be! Oh, you will have your difficulties,"** they laughed. **"Things will happen,"** they threw up their hands as if to say, 'Well, what do you expect?' **"That is part of your growth. But no more burden and no more of the burdensome bearing of weight."**

They regarded me seriously and then their expressions turned mischievous. **"*We* do the giving,"** they said. **"*You* do the living."** I recognized this line. It was from an old Elvis Presley song! My eyes widened as I stared at them and they broke into delighted laughter. I barely got out the words, "You're amazing, Grandmothers," before they grew serious again. **"Let us give through you,"** they said. **"And enjoy!**

"This way of giving will fill you with pleasure. You will feel our presence and our love pouring through you. Then there will be no more depletion from giving. The old way of giving," they shook their heads in disgust, **"where woman especially was designated as the giver and was at the same time cut off from her own source of supply exhausted her."** Pausing, deep in thought they said, **"That is not the true way to live and give. *You Are Not Cut Off!* You are part of the source.**

"You are a jeweled facet of the source," they said, **"manifesting wherever you are. Think of yourself as the pitcher pouring forth, and know that the supply is never ending."** Wagging their fingers they said, **"Do not go around heedlessly giving. Don't even *think* of giving.**

"Instead open to us; open always to us. Ask for everything you need. It will be given to you," they promised, **"and then what you give will go out from you effortlessly, and with joy."**

"Thank you, Grandmothers," I bowed. **"We thank *you*,"** they said. "Why are they thanking me?" I mumbled and they explained how **"At** one" they are with each one they call **"the jeweled facets. We are grateful for each facet of the Divine who is coming forth at this time to do our work on earth."**

Thrilled by this concept of effortless giving, I wanted to know about these so-called **"jeweled facets."** They would say no more, however, and the drumbeat changed, signaling my return.

CHAPTER 7

Feminine Power is a Fearsome Thing

"Because you are a human being you have a limited comprehension of 'masculine' and 'feminine' power. "

Full of questions, I was always puzzling over something the Grandmothers had said or shown me. By this time I had passed their empowerment on to three groups of women and was wondering if this was the best way to get their message out. I was also curious about what they called *"effortless giving."* There was so much I wanted to know and while each journey answered some questions, it brought up others.

Eagle was on my left as we flew upward and rising in formation (even though there were only two of us,) he let me lead. "Eagle, why are you male?" I said as I glanced over my shoulder. "The Grandmothers work is mostly about women, so why are you a 'he'?" **"Because I am, "** he said.

Maybe I needed his male strength to master this task of flight, or his fighting spirit to do this work. Whatever it was, he wouldn't say more.

We approached the Grandmothers' circle and hovered high above it, and then I came in fast. Banking at the last minute, I looked like a cartoon figure with my wings above my head as my talons touched ground.

I landed lightly and, proud of myself, strutted toward them just as Eagle did. Chuckling at my behavior, I happened to tip my head forward and notice my body. What was this? My chest and stomach were hard and flat, a penis lay against one leg and my legs were straight and strong, rooting themselves in large, solid feet. Nothing about this body was rounded or soft. I was in male form.

I felt different too—resolute, forceful and impatient; I could feel my eagerness to engage. I was male, just like Eagle. This frightened me until I remembered that everything that took place on a journey was part of some learning. "Wait!" I said as I thought about this, "Am I male, or am I simply embodying masculine power?

"Grandmothers," I cried, and as soon as I called, they stood before me in their eagle bodies. "What is this male power I have? What does carrying masculine power have to do with the work of empowering woman?"

"Because you are a human being you have a limited comprehension of what "masculine" and "feminine" power are," they said. **"Because humans don't know what these terms really mean, all you do with "male," "female," "masculine" and "feminine" is categorize."** They smiled; amused by my ignorance as again I surveyed my body. "Teach me, Grandmothers. Teach me about the real power in woman."

"It is a fearsome thing," they said, **"feminine power is a serious thing."** Shaking their heads, they said, **"It is not the way you think of it here on earth—deferential, coquettish and manipulative. It is none of these,"** they exclaimed in disgust. **"It is a force of tremendous DIGNITY."** From the queenly way they held themselves, I saw their feelings about this. "It's time for me to acquire some of this dignity too," I thought, "so I can do a better job of passing on their message."

Now, as a woman I stood tall and confident before them. This 'me' was graceful, sure in her movements, speech, and above all in her purpose. I had never thought of myself as dignified. **"Get used to it,"** they laughed, **"This is your destiny."**

Smiling, joking, they reassured me, **"You can still have fun—it's not joy-killing; it's dignified, always dignified, even in play. Dignity has to do with the sacredness of the being that you are."** Fastening their eyes on mine, they commanded: **"Never, NEVER forget!** *That* **is what you are."**

"Grandmothers," I said, "I assume I am to spread your teachings and your empowerment, the things you've told me, as you are now. Is this right?" **"Yes,"** they said, twelve eagle heads nodding.

"I've worked with groups of women as you know." **"That is fine for now,"** they said, **"it's building. The swell will carry you, and you will know your direction. The swell will teach you."**

"Should I offer this to women on an on-going basis?" **"Yes, yes,"** they answered with enthusiasm, **"and let it build. That is the way. The word will spread."**

They stood back, inspecting me, and my eyes followed theirs. I looked down to check on my body and saw that I was now my usual female self, and when I hurriedly glanced up I saw that they too had shed their eagle bodies. "Hum," I mused. "These bodies are like costumes, useful for making a point or illustrating an experience." The Grandmothers smiled and nodded. Then they drew me to themselves and placing their hands over my heart, lifted my chest as they said, **"High hearted."**

I tilted my head to see what they were doing, and saw light shining off the front of me, shooting outward from my heart! The supply of light seemed to be coming from theirs.

"The high heart, they said, as they filled my heart with light from their own. "Oh...now I feel it," I gasped as power suffused my chest, swelled me open like a flower in bloom. In radiant display, light shot back and forth between us. It was a two way broadcast of light and power—from my heart to theirs and from theirs back to mine.

"I want to believe in Self more, Grandmothers—capital S," I said. "Within this body," I pointed to myself, "I want to believe in Self. I want confidence in my thoughts, in my appearance, in everything. Please help me." They clustered around, touching me here and there, straightening and elongating my spine and said, **"The dignity of bearing is important."**

I watched as they filed ahead of me, each Grandmother carrying something heavy on her head. They were showing me how to carry a burden with grace and I followed them, mimicking their movements as I too carried water in an urn on my head. **"The straight spine makes it easier,"** they said as they glanced back. **"Remember this."**

I looked up from the pathway for a moment and when I looked down again there were no more urns and our arms and hands were free. Immediately we began to laugh, and whirling, commenced a dance. But as I reveled in the welcome feeling of lightness, the drumbeat changed. Quickly the dancing stopped, and I turned and bowed my leave.

CHAPTER 8

You Must Grow into Your Spirit

"We are showing you the energy of yang as it is on earth...entirely out of control."

I was still living in two worlds—the world of non-ordinary reality with the Grandmothers, and the daily life of home, clients, and friends. I was noticing, however, that the differences between these realities no longer seemed as stark. Although I didn't mention the Grandmothers to my clients or to most or my friends, by now the Grandmothers' teachings had permeated my life. The energy of yin had begun to expand my heart and soften my hard edges. I was now less prone to anger, more open with everyone.

Most of the time I was high on the Grandmothers' work, but there were times when it felt like too much information, too much change, just plain *too much* for me and at these times I found myself longing for a "normal" life.

I first experienced this after I had worked with the Grandmothers for several months. After journeying almost daily, I became overwhelmed by the amount of information I was receiving and began to slack off my three to one schedule, journeying only when I felt up to it.

Working in the dimension of non-ordinary reality was fascinating, but hard work. Some journeys brought up memories and feelings I hadn't known I'd had. When this occurred, the states of consciousness that surfaced took me a while to process. Other journeys were so filled with unorthodox ideas and images that my mind rebelled against the strangeness of it all. I might try to gain control of my experiences by pigeonholing the Grandmothers' lessons—a fruitless endeavor if ever there was one.

There was no one with whom I could share all this. After a few fitful attempts, I realized that until I truly understood what the Grandmothers were teaching me, no one else could understand it either. Even my spiritual friends didn't get this stuff unless and until I first became clear. My husband wasn't interested in such far out experiences, so I was living in a private, multi-dimensional world where I still had to look and act like a normal person.

Attempting to slow this process was like trying to push a wave back to the ocean. Whenever I felt overwhelmed by the work and stopped journeying, the Grandmothers popped into my awareness, nudged and taught me as I went about my day. Bear showed up in my dreams. I continued to hold non-ordinary reality at bay until the day I remembered what I had said when the astrologer had told me about the work that was coming to me; "If I give in to my fear of the unknown I will never forgive myself." I couldn't quit.

If I could clearly differentiate my own thoughts from the messages I was receiving from Spirit, maybe I wouldn't feel so overwhelmed by whatever came up on a journey. I wanted to be more objective, not so personally affected by this work.

As I began my next visit to the upper world I looked like the statue in the Albuquerque airport of the shaman holding on to an eagle. For some reason this time I didn't even consider flying on my own. Instead, my arms reached up to Eagle's feet, held on, and as he sprang into the air my body arced and my grip tightened. "I have been pretty fatigued lately," I told myself, "that must be it."

Eagle took me all the way to the Grandmothers like this. When we glided above their circle he let me down gently and I glimpsed a look of compassion in his eyes. "Something must be wrong with me today," I thought, "Eagle never looks at me like that."

I crouched before them in an almost fetal position and gasped, "Grandmothers, my spirit has been wounded, Eagle has shown me this." I spoke the words before I thought the thought. My spirit *had* been wounded. This was what Eagle had seen.

I glanced down at myself and saw that once again I was in male form. This time, however, I was a wounded Indian brave with a bare chest and a breechclout.

The Grandmothers took a long, hard look at me and said, **"You try to do too much. Wait. You must grow into your spirit."** I was no longer to do anything on my own. "Grandmothers, I sobbed, "I want to let you lead, not struggle and try so hard. I want to operate from spirit, outward." Gazing at me with wise eyes they said, **"You cannot fly so high any other way."**

I heard the truth in this and asked, "What *is* the best way to use what you have given me?" **"Just sit with it in silence,"** they said. **"Wait. The next wave will come from within you but you must wait for it. Now is the time for building your reserves, then there will be more for you to give.**

"THE WORK SHOULD BE EFFORTLESS," they said. **"If it is not effortless, it is not *us* working, but your mind.** "The work," I realized, meant not only this, but *all* work.

"By the ease of work you will know whether it is Spirit working through you or only your mind manufacturing. The best use you can make of what we have given you is to embody our lessons. That is the highest, deepest and best use and from that will come all else. Do not seek after anything, but wait.

"Know your body," they said, **"your body is your compass. Both physical and emotional feelings are registered in the body. There is wholeness, a groundedness in this way of perceiving that is more reliable than the mind. You will FEEL the truth!**

"The mind doesn't particularly produce a feeling," they said, **"rather it contracts with doubt and worry; it says many words and shows pictures, but there is no true feeling in it."** As I reflected on their words, I realized this was an accurate description of my mind. **"Trust the feeling,"** they said. **"How do you feel? It is quite simple."**

Their words became a touchstone, a mantra. I found it easier to keep my mind clear, to stay in touch with myself if I remembered to ask myself, "How do you feel?"

After a brief silence I said, "Grandmothers, can you tell me anything about the headache I have? Asking, "How do you feel?" had put me in touch with the pain in my head. They were silent, so I continued, "Is there something that will help me cope with or release this pain?"

I was hoping they would tell me the cause of my headaches, a deep-seated attitude or a traumatic event, something that would make this chronic pain understandable. "I'm willing to do whatever it takes to clear this from my body," I said. Several minutes passed while I waited.

I was about to give up when they came forward, and reached in with their hands to open up my body. When I saw my skull, my spine and where the two attached I whispered, "There's something there that doesn't look like a body part." Fascinated, I watched them work, and saw that whatever it was, this thing was attached to my spine. Before I could ask about it they said, **"You are doing the right things."** My diet was good, I was getting exercise, bodywork, and I was meditating. "Yes," I said, "but I still have pain."

"Oh," I cried as I saw a row of hooks dug into the flesh and bone of my spinal column. The Grandmothers were pulling on them, loosening those along the right side. As they did this a stabbing sensation ran up and down my back. The flesh there, caught by these hooks was red and inflamed. "Oh, thank God," I cried, as they covered my back with a steaming poultice.

"Must I be attached to those hooks?" I whimpered. **"We can do no more now,"** they said; **"it is not yet time for the release."** They wiped away my tears and reassured me, **"it will come."** "But Grandmothers, how do I cope with the pain until the release comes?" **"We are here,"** they said as they cradled me in their arms.

Comfortable in their embrace, I felt the sun flooding warmth and light over us and at last I grew calm. They had said my release would come, and I believed them.

When I happened to glance down at my body I saw that I was back in eagle form. "Hum-m-m-m," I mused, "when I came today I was a male, wounded and broken, and now I'm an eagle. Grandmothers, why was I a man when I came?" **"You were totally yang,"** they said; **"yang energy had run you to the point of exhaustion."** All my trying, my worry about doing things right—this was what they meant. Those were symptoms of excessive yang, and I had had them a long time. No wonder I had looked the way I did.

They walked me to the edge of their circle and pointed into the distance where I saw something moving. Dust flew up, creating a cloud that traveled with it, and as I drew closer I made out an animal of some kind, tied to a stake. Straining against its tether, it threw up a cloud of dust as it galloped back and forth.

I didn't want to get too close to it, but from where I stood it looked like a wild bull. Panting and frothing at the mouth, it bolted from side to side, jerked against its leash while steam rose off its back.

It appeared at the same time terrifying and exhausted. Each time it flung itself away from the stake, the rawhide strip stretched further and the tether pulled tighter. This had obviously been going on for some time because by now the rope barely held.

As I wondered why the Grandmothers were showing me this, they said, **"The energy of yang is running amok. We are showing you the**

energy of yang as it is today." The bull flinging itself against the confines of its leash represented yang. Crazed, a wild look in its eyes, it thundered past and I jumped back. As the Grandmothers signaled me to stand behind them, they said, **"Yang is entirely out of control."**

We stood together while again the beast flung itself as far as it could, thundered back the way it had come and again raced for the end of the rope. **"There is no force in the world strong enough to counter-balance this out-of-control energy of yang,"** they said. **"Yin is depleted and unable to counter yang, which has become increasingly wild and violent. And human beings who live in these times of gross imbalance have come to believe that life is like this—filled with violent excesses. Due to yin/yang imbalance and yang dominance, your view of life has become distorted, causing you to believe in the inevitability of violence.**

"Yin," they crooned, **"is wait. Yin is hold,"** they sang, their voices dropping on 'hold.' **"Yin is a container, a container we can fill. We will fill you."** When I came to them today I was a broken male, exhausted from trying too hard. Under my breath I muttered, "This is what I need—to let them fill me." The crazed bull energy of yang had run me to exhaustion.

"Do not go off on your own now," they said, **"trying to do things by yourself. That is the old way,"** they shook their heads in disgust. And fixing me with a serious look they said, **"Let *us* fill you."**

As I sat on the dais in my eagle body, I felt so much better than I did when I began the journey. Now I could move my head and wings; already I had regained some strength. Without my even asking it, the Grandmothers had answered my question of how to distinguish the messages of my mind from their messages. I must attend to my feelings.

"Grandmothers," I said, "it feels so good to be strong again, to sit solidly planted. Thank you," I bowed my feathered head. " And thank you, Eagle," I turned to acknowledge my escort and friend.

On my way back to ordinary reality I thought about this journey. It was my mind that had whipped me into efforts that I could see were pointless, and seeing this pointlessness had sapped my energy and confidence. Like the bull, my mind, without purpose or meaningful direction, too had been tethered. Yang had driven me like the bull in races of effort and despair, wounding my heart that needed only to receive. This was the tyranny of yang energy at work. I knew it well. I had lived in it all my life. But I didn't want to any more.

CHAPTER 9

The Net of Light

"This is the Net that will hold the earth together."

I was tired of the painful excesses of yang and had to find a way to ground myself in the energy of yin, but how? This was the question for my next journey, but as I stood before the Grandmothers, prepared to ask it, **they spoke instead. "Cherish the daughters and sons as you cherish the Mother,"** they said, **"all are her children. Pass this on, to the younger ones, the older ones, to others who don't have it. Pass it on."**

I assumed the first sentence meant I was to love all people as I loved God the Mother, as all are her children, part of the same family. But **"Pass this on?"** The Grandmothers ignored my puzzled expression and continued to speak with authority.

I simply listened and watched, as before me appeared two sisters who had come to an empowerment ceremony last month. Although I knew that these two were now in India, I saw them as clearly as if they were sitting in front of me. Bea wore a blue dress and smiled her broad smile while Peggy, standing slightly behind her, cocked her head and gave me an impish grin as if to say, "I bet you didn't expect this." A filament of light connected them to me and me to them. **"This is the thread of light that connects all the women who have received our empowerment,"** the Grandmothers said.

I watched as they brought forward each woman to whom I had passed their empowerment. Spread on the ground before us was a lighted net. Each one stood at a point on the net, positioned at a juncture where the strands of light came together, forming a cross or x. The net spread far into the distance and appeared to be held steady and lit by these women.

Other people were also present on the Net of Light, but they were further out and I couldn't see their faces. The Grandmothers said, **"Together you form a web, a Net of Light. This is a network, a lov-**

ing Net, and all are family in this Net." Standing tall, like the queens they were, they proclaimed, **"This is the Net that will hold the earth together. The Net,"** they repeated, **"that will hold the earth together."**

This was the same Net of Light they had spoken of earlier. One of their pivotal teachings, the Net of Light provides a way to support one another and support the earth. The light that moves along its strands is a visual demonstration of love; within the Net light and love are synonymous. Because the Net works directly with love, as we connect with it, we become instruments for positive change on earth.

For the first few years, only women gathered to do the Grandmothers' work. But as men began to come to our meetings, the Grandmothers gave me the cloak of comfort ceremony to pass on to them, so that men as well as women could become part of the Net of Light, and take part in infusing the energy of yin back into the planet.

Activating the Net of Light at this point in history is essential as it is a band of energy, a metaphor for loving connection that holds and upholds the earth. As I gazed at the network of crossing lines before me the Grandmothers said, **"Meditate on this Net of Light. Use it to support one another, to support the earth, and to strengthen the energy of yin on the planet.**

"Do not take seemingly small activities like this for granted," they said. **"Every change in human consciousness, no matter how insignificant it may seem to you, carries with it wide reaching implications."**

"Grandmothers, what a gift you are giving," I said. **"It is *our* gift,"** they said and from the emphasis on "our" I understood that they generously included all in this act of giving." **It is *our* gift to one another and to *HER*, whom we all embody."**

As they said, **"*Her* whom we all embody,"** the presence of God/Goddess, the Beloved joined us. The air shimmered as waves of power washed me and suddenly, though I was still journeying with the Grandmothers, I was also in India with Bea and Peggy. *I was everywhere.* The Grandmothers' phrase, **"Covers the earth,"** came to me as I felt myself at one with Gaia, the great Earth Mother, swelling until, enormous of body, with endless wings or arms (I don't know which) I cradled the earth close to my heart.

The tenderness and love I felt was almost painful. "I can't hold this glory in my body, Grandmothers," I sobbed. **"Enjoy this gift you have been given,"** they said, eyes full of love. **"Take joy in it."** I had never seen such a look.

At last I calmed down, and spent the rest of the journey soaking in that love, so full of it that when the drumbeat changed and I made my way back to ordinary reality my body trembled and seemed to glow. I was so deeply content that I was speechless for the rest of the day.

"The work of the Net of Light is done through you. All good and goodness flow though this."

After a few journeys to the lower world I returned to learn more about the Net of Light. The Grandmothers had told me to "pass it on" but how?

Today they were in human form and after placing me in their midst, they directed me to turn in a circle, a few degrees at a time. As I rotated, each Grandmother filled me with power, broadcasting it into my back, front and sides until I thrummed with energy.

"**Each person is a jewel in the Net of Light,**" they said, "**and helps hold the Net together.**" Again I saw the women to whom I had passed their empowerment. They seemed to glow, and behind them stood rows and rows of people. As I watched, the Grandmothers said, "**This shimmering in the Net that you see is jewel light.**

"**Know the reality of this Net, for by knowing it and being at one with it you do untold good.**" I listened. "**Without thought, without effort, without awareness that it is happening, but just by being at one with the power of the Net of Light, you do untold good.**

"**First think of the Net of Light, and then think of yourself as a shimmering point of light on the Net. This will give you peace, joy, and belief in Self, capital S!**" they said.

"**The work of the Net of Light is done through you, it is done silently. The brain does not control this. This work is done through the jewel within your heart, through the *Being* that you are. All good and goodness flow from this.**

"**You are connected to us and to one another through the Net of Light,**" they said. "**Take joy in that. It is a special blessing to be part of this Net, and no accident.**" They showed me that I was to pass the Net of Light on to others in the form of a guided meditation.

Moved by the generosity of this Net, I was also shaken by the power of its potential. The Grandmothers had never spoken more eloquently and my eyes were wide while my mouth hung open in awe.

Laughing, they poked gentle fun at the way I continued to revere them and teased me about how I still saw myself as the child and they the adults. Shaking their heads, as if to say, "When are you going to get over this?" they flooded me with love.

"The great plenitude of the universe wants a place to manifest, and it can only do so in an open heart."

After I had passed the Net of Light on to several groups and we had practiced casting the Net to those around the world who yearn for connection several women asked me, "Can men be members of the Net of Light?" I didn't know the answer to this, but the Grandmothers would.

"**Not many men will be drawn to the concept of a Net of Light,**" they said. "**If they are, they are welcome, but only men who already carry a balance of yin and yang within themselves will be drawn to this and there are not many of these,**" they said. "**What upholds the Net is mostly the energy of yin within women. Men are welcome to the Net,**" they said, "**but such men will be rare.**" Men, by nature, are more yang, while women are more yin. Since the Net of Life is itself a yin (nurturing, supportive) construct and women hold within themselves more yin than yang, it is easier for women to relate to the Net of Light.

"**When you send light out on the Net, send primarily to women,**" the Grandmothers said. "**The Net's primary function is to support the structure of the earth while its secondary function is to save and support individuals.**" They explained, "**Since women care most about the Net, believe in and will act on it, cast to them first.**

"**To most men the Net of Light seems only an idea. Since they don't understand it, they won't act on it. All men will benefit from the Net, as will every form of life, but when you cast the Net, focus primarily on women.**" I heard the rightness, the economy in what they were saying. For a yin construct (the Net of Light) to operate efficiently one needed a yin operator (a woman.)

"Is there more you want to say about the Net of Light, so I can explain it," I asked. "**Trust that giving is always receiving,**" they said. "***Giving from the heart*** **always leads to further reception. Other kinds of 'giving' are not giving at all; only from the heart do we give.**

"**The universe supports an open heart. The universe** *waits* **for an open heart. The great plenitude of the universe wants a place to manifest, and it can only do so in an open heart.**" They shook their heads in wonder. "**You have no idea how much rejoicing there is in** heaven when one heart opens. Instantly the great plenitude rushes in to fill that heart."

With passion, they said, "**So much more would be given to you, so** *much, much* **more if you would but open! It is like priming a pump. If you pour out but a little of the water of your heart, a gusher will well back to you.**" Laughing they said, "**No one understands this.**" And holding their sides in mirth, they took delight in the surprise in store for us once we figure this out.

"**Your heart receives a gift when it gives through the Net of Light and this gift comes to you via your senses. It may come as the touch of a breeze, the embrace of a friend, the scent of flowers, sea, or pine. Beautiful colors, sights, sounds, and tastes—oh, so many gifts are given to you. You have no idea,**" they laughed. "**Pay attention,**" they said, "**these gifts are legion.**"

Their flood of information overwhelmed me but they weren't finished yet. "**At this moment you live within the great plenitude,**" they said. "**This is,**" they paused, searching for the right word…"**a secret. It has** *become* **a secret,**" they corrected themselves. "**No one recognizes that at this moment all live within the great plenitude.**" Looking into my eyes they urged me/us, "**Open your hearts! Give! Send light, that more may rush to you.**"

"These meditations ensure that the work we give goes into the viscera, into the body/mind and is held there, becoming truth."

"When I asked what else they wanted me to pass on they said, "**We will give meditations and visualizations to anchor our teachings. These ensure that the work we give you goes into the viscera, into the body/mind and is held there, becoming truth. This truth,**" they said, "**will be deeply known, not something that only passes through the mind.**

"**The Net of Light is an example of such a meditation. Begin to visualize it as a lighted fish net, its strands held by the being of each one. Not by her conscious effort, but by her very being. "The women who have had the empowerment and the men who have received the cloak of comfort hold the Net most brightly. From them it spreads to others.**

"**The Net of Light creates a paradigm shift, a shift in consciousness that will go on to become a shift in matter. The light that goes out from each person dives downward into the earth and spreads**

everywhere." As they spoke, I saw it happen. The more people took hold of it, the brighter the Net of Light glowed. It was just as the Grandmothers had said; its strands spread out and covered the world.

"You will feel the sparkling effervescence of the Net of Light inside your veins and experience light pouring from your hearts. The light that is sent from your hearts will return to you through your eyes, ears and breath." As they spoke, energy began to flood outward from my heart and at the same time there was an awakening sensation in my eyes and ears. My breathing deepened.

For several minutes all I heard was this deep breathing and then they said, **"Giving and receiving through the Net of Light is a tremendous experience."** Often they had spoken of expansion and a few times they had given me a taste of it, but what I felt now was beyond this. As I looked outward I saw people's souls reaching throughout the world in a way I could never have imagined. I could also feel my own expansion. Connected and all knowing, my body fanned out and covered the universe.

I was so thrilled by what I was perceiving that I wanted everyone to share in it. "People could draw the Net, or even dance it," I thought. "That would make it more real to them." Immediately I was flooded with thoughts and images of people writing, singing, and dancing. "Are these the Grandmothers' thoughts, or mine?" I wondered, and heard their response: **"Is there any difference?"**

Shaking my head, I looked up to see them chuckling. Then they reached over and patted my back, saying, **"This group with whom you are working will deepen; they will gain in power."** Heads nodding judiciously, they said, **"They will do good—on many, many levels. Levels they have no idea of. This,"** they said, **"is the potential of the Net of Light,"** and they laughingly confirmed that it was indeed they, the Grandmothers, speaking.

"The Net is anchored in each one," they said, **"and the process of holding the earth has already begun. It is not necessary that you *do* anything. There is no responsibility about this work—only to enjoy it. And those who wish to participate more in it will enjoy more.**

"Those who do this work," they smiled, **"will grow in joy. They will embody joy."** With or without assistance the Grandmothers would bring about the needed energy shift on earth. Those who chose to take part in this work would have the joy of participating in saving our planet.

"Grandmothers," I said, "before I leave I must ask something. I am still afraid of coming out with your message. Please help me." They began to talk among themselves, and then turned to me.

"Dissolving the fear of dissolving," they said, "relates to owning the expansiveness of one's being. Such expansion automatically removes fear because fear itself is contraction. Fear is the state of being caught in the small self."

As I labored to understand what they had said they drew themselves up to their full height. "It is your identification with your small self that creates your fear," they said. "When you realize this, fear will simply go. The 'dissolving' of this small, fearful self will happen during the process of expansion; conversely, the process of expansion will occur as the small self dissolves." As my consciousness expanded, fear and worry would fade; as my fear faded, my consciousness would expand.

"The wings now spread farther, wider and higher," they said, and I felt myself back in my eagle body, attention on my wings that now began to beat, pulling me upright. As they opened, I noticed that they expanded my heart. "Feel that!" the Grandmothers said, "Embody that!"

I realized that whenever I became aware of the presence of fear I could think of opening and expanding my wings, my heart. If I closed my eyes and remembered my great Self, my eagle self, and instead of fighting fear or worry I simply held to this *Self*, my little self would soon dissolve. My old belief that I *was* this little self lay at the bottom of all my fear.

As I breathed deeply, I heard myself say, "I am the bird with the ah-h-h...bright wings!" A mythical creature, there was now no limit to my reach. "Fanning out, out and *O-u-t*," I crooned," as I watched my wings span mountains and valleys.

In ecstasy, I soared until the drumbeat changed. This brought my feet back to ground and standing before the Grandmothers I bowed low, turned to Eagle and began my descent. The sense of expansion, of being this great Self, continued long after I returned to ordinary reality, taking me days to literally come down.

The Net of Light meditation anchors the Grandmothers' work on earth. I had to journey to them several times to understand it well enough to pass it on, but at last I called together those who had received their empowerment and shared it with them. From that time on, they formed a group; coming together regularly to practice whatever teachings the Grandmothers gave. In time this core group grew from the first eleven who received the Grandmothers' empowerment to over a hundred.

Note: Several years later, thousands of women and many men have been gifted with the Grandmothers' Empowerment and cloak of comfort and at this point there are Grandmothers' groups all over the world.

The group in Laguna Beach is made up of all ages; the youngest is in her twenties while the oldest is in her eighties. Most of the women and men are in the middle of their lives. Although many women have received the Grandmothers' empowerment and a lesser number of men have received the cloak of comfort, most of them are scattered across the globe. But those who live near by have become a regular part of the Grandmothers' work. After the empowerment ceremony some went through dramatic changes while others experienced subtler, often more pervasive change. It has been a great thrill for me to observe their growth.

The Grandmothers say, **"Group work anchors our teaching for everyone on earth, infusing the energy of yin more deeply into the planet."** The work of this group has benefited not only them, but everyone.

Soon after they received the empowerment people began to tell me of changes taking place in their lives. Mary, for example, had just turned forty when she came to her first Grandmothers' meeting. For five years she had tried to get pregnant and shared with us her longing for a baby as well as her despair at her lack of success. A month later, while I was addressing announcements for our next meeting, she called to tell me that she was pregnant. "I never believed in miracles before, but the Grandmothers have performed one this time," she crowed. Eight months later she delivered a baby boy.

Mary had her baby, Carolyn began her first healthy relationship with a man and Lori found the right career. Michael, a brilliant scientist, awakened to his heart as well as his brain and began to work on an invention to benefit humanity. There were so many success stories, each one following on the heels of an empowerment ceremony.

Stories like these can sound simplistic but the truth was, after receiving the empowerment from the Grandmothers we *did* change. We saw it in ourselves, in one another, and each time we gathered we delighted in sharing our joy. Miracles were happening and happening fast. But no matter how the "miracle" might appear, the common thread in each was an increased confidence in Self. Early on the Grandmothers had said, **"Each person is not just a small and limited self but is part of something much greater."** This "Self," was something we were coming to know.

Connie, a soft-spoken woman with a creative mind, strongly registered this increase in Self-confidence. An accomplished painter, before receiving the Grandmothers' empowerment she had a tendency to apologize for her work. At our first meeting she was so soft spoken I could hardly hear her. But after six months with the Grandmothers, she informed us, "I'm better at my work now than ever.

"My perception of my art is different and my perception of life is also different. Since the Grandmothers came into my life I respond more positively to everything; even though my life's 'trials and tribulations' have remained much the same, *I am different*." Looking at her, we could not help but agree. The Grandmothers had promised that as we opened to the energy of yin, our life would become easier. This seemed to be happening.

Lucille tells this story of how the Grandmothers responded to her. "Shortly after receiving their empowerment and before I knew much about them, I began to feel a free-floating depression. Since I was hardly ever depressed, this was unusual, especially because there was nothing in my life to cause it. I kept poring over everything that had gone on in my life, but I couldn't figure out where this heavy feeling was coming from.

"After the depression had dragged on a few days, I was walking along the beach and just sat down on the sand and called on the Grandmothers. I remember saying, "I don't know if you're real or not but if you're listening, take this away!" I didn't care why the depression had come up; I just wanted it gone. As soon as I asked, I felt different. It was a physical feeling I had, of the depression being gone, and it happened almost immediately. It is now two years later and it has never returned."

Ann says, "Right after our baby was born my husband lost his job and suddenly we were in dire financial straits. That was the day Sandra and told me about the Grandmothers and that's how I happened to come.

"Right after the empowerment ceremony I started to communicate with the Grandmothers. I felt funny asking for something material at such a spiritual occasion and I wasn't sure if this was the right thing to do, but because my family desperately needed rescuing, I asked anyway.

"I went home from that meeting feeling peaceful and the next day from out of the blue my husband and I got some new ideas for a brochure for his business. We put it together and no sooner did we send it out than the money started rolling in. Our whole financial situation turned around within two to three weeks. Although I'll never be sure exactly why our fortune so quickly reversed itself, all I can attribute it to is the Grandmothers."

Each person quickly developed their own relationship with the Grandmothers. Rich feels all the Grandmothers standing around him in his office, especially when he is working with a patient. For some people a particular Grandmother might consistently appear. Stephanie, for example, has a Black Grandmother who is always with her while Helga's Grandmother looks like a Native American. Stephanie is not black nor is Helga Native American—it just worked out that way. Some feel the presence of two or three Grandmothers around them while others have a sense of the whole group; for some the Grandmothers' presence is clear while for others it is vague. They are *present*, however. That we all agree.

Sharing such profound experiences brought a feeling of closeness to the group. After our meditation I urge everyone to remain quiet and keep their focus inward but most can't do it. The joy that bubbles up in them is irrepressible. It is hard for them to leave these meetings, and gangs of them to out to lunch together, prolonging their good feelings as long as possible. My husband once asked me why people keep returning to these meetings. When I took his question to the group, they said, "It fills me," "It's like church, only better," "It's the love," "The Grandmothers have changed me."

Although the importance of people's connection through the Net of Light cannot be overstated perhaps it is most clearly brought home by Shirley's story. Shirley, a member of the core group, had just returned from the hospital when I happened to telephone her one morning. Even though she was still weak and recovering from hypothermia, she wanted to tell me about what had happened to her.

She had taken her ten-year-old son and a friend camping during a hot spell, and when they drove into their campground she noticed people floating on the river beside the camp. So as soon as they got out of the car they grabbed their inner tubes and ran down to the water.

The three of them were lazing their way down river, laughing and bouncing over tiny rapids but mostly just drifting with the current until they came upon a tree that had been submerged by spring flooding. A submerged tree is a dangerous object in a river, a fact Shirley hadn't known, and although the boys floated past it, before she realized what was happening to her the current sucked her float under.

The force that pushed her down pinned her against the limbs of the tree for what seemed an eternity. When at last she found an opening between branches, the pressure of the water against the tree kept her locked there. She had her head up and she could breathe, but she couldn't move.

When he discovered his mother missing her son climbed out of the water and when he saw her head bob up he ran down the bank to try to save her. Fearing he too would get dragged under, she yelled at the boys to run to the road for help. Meanwhile she treaded water and waited.

The water was snowmelt and though it was now midsummer, it felt like ice, so cold that when she couldn't free her legs she realized she might not make it. The shock must have numbed her mind as well as her body because when she tried to meditate or pray she couldn't concentrate enough to do either. But she could think of the core group that she had been working with for months. "This is what held me up," she says. "I thought of my connection to all of you through the Net of Light.

"The entire time I was in the water a calming presence was there with me. This eliminated any fear I normally would have had. I was surprised at the time that I was so calm. It was simple. I couldn't focus on anything else. All I could think of was this group and the Net of Light. That was it. After you came to mind, I felt connected and after that I just surrendered to whatever would happen." She waited in the freezing water, knowing she might die, yet not afraid, until rescue workers pulled her from the river.

I cried when she told me what had happened to her, tears of gratitude to the Grandmothers who had given us this miraculous tool. Her connection to the Net of Light had dissolved her fear; it had given her peace at a time of extreme difficulty. I share Shirley's story because it shows both the power of the Net of Light and the intense bond it creates between those who use it.

CHAPTER 10

It is Time for Yin and Yang to Move

"At this time the vision of mankind is obscured. Many live in fear."

Even though I knew with absolute certainty the truth of whatever the Grandmothers said I kept getting in my own way. Shortly after the reports from the core group I plunged into doubt again. "I'm glad these women are experiencing the power and peace of the Grandmothers," I said to myself, "but they are just a few." My mind now minimized the value of the work I had been doing.

These downturns into doubt were becoming frequent. Although there was no reason for me to feel negative about the Grandmothers' work, I was. Why? I searched my mind for the cause, but couldn't find it.

I decided to lay this problem before the Grandmothers, but as I flew upward, I realized that it was the holy man I really wanted to see. "He's been with me a long time," I said, "like a father, only better."

As soon as this thought came I looked around, and there he stood. But rather than welcome me, he seemed to glower, and before I could say a word, he grabbed my hand and marched me to the edge of a cliff. Pointing into the distance he said, **"Look!"**

I looked but didn't see much of anything, just a mass of darkness. With gray clouds overhead, a dark land lay before me. The smoke and clouds that hung in the air obscured everything. **"This,"** he said, **"is the darkness that covers and threatens to further cover the earth. And *this*,"** he stabbed his finger at it, **"is the darkness that threatens to cover you!"** Giving me a look of frightening severity, he said, **"You are losing sight of your purpose."**

"What?" I stammered, but he would say no more. "Please, no!" I cried, terrified, and immediately heard, **"CUT IT AWAY!"** as a knife hurtled down from above my head and a dark mass fell off to the left side of my body and another to the right. A pile of darkness had been attached to me at the center of my chest!

The holy man had made a cut at my sternum, just at the skin, and pulled it off—left and right. "Oh, my God," I whimpered, "I never thought of anything like this. I assumed I had done something wrong, that's why I came today. I thought *I* had caused my own discouragement, assumed it was my wrong attitude, my something...."

"No, no," he said, showing me that what I had thought '*my*' discouragement had really been this dark mass. I shook, as I watched, never having dreamed such a horror possible. Calmly, he straightened and strengthened my spine. **"Must have backbone,"** he said. **"Too many doubts.**

"At this time it is difficult to maintain faith without falling into doubt." The mass of grayness I had seen assured that. The discouragement and doubt I had felt were not personal. As I remembered the black thing that had been attached to my chest, I started shaking again.

I watched as he peeled the remains of it off my back and saw that it resembled a heavy cloak. "That is why it's been hard for me to reach people with this message," I said. "I've been weighted down." Then I realized that those I had hoped to reach had also been weighed down. *Everyone* was covered by this gray stuff.

As he lifted more layers off my back what relief I felt. **"You must let your light shine,"** he said, and when I looked down I *was* shining. Light, growing brighter by the moment, was pouring off the back and front of me. **"Too much darkness for too long,"** he said.

Brightness and a vibrating shimmer seeped through my skin and moved outward until I glowed and hummed. While I reveled in this, the meeting I was to attend that night came to mind. **"Go tonight,"** he said, **"and be a light. Wherever you go, now you carry this light.**

"Mankind's vision is obscured at this time and many live in fear. The light within them is actually great," he said, **"but the light one sees coming from them is small.**

"Do not look to others," he said, speaking through me to everyone. Since most people are unaware of their own light, they would also be unaware of mine. Therefore we could not look to one another for confirmation. We must turn to the light within us, not to the darkness obscuring the world around us. **"Look to the Divine. What did you ever gain by holding back?"** he prodded me towards courage. **"What good ever came from hiding in the dark?**

"Step Into The Light Now! Do not be a child whining to see me, whining for my approval. Step into the light and *own it*! Own the verticality of this power," he said, demonstrating how calling on light pulled me to my full height. Standing tall, my body was pulsing.

The force of light filled me and I straightened and aligned with it. "This is my nature," I thought; it's *everyone's* nature. "How can we *know* when we are in tune, when we are living according to divine guidance?" I asked. "**Walk tall,**" he said. "**When you walk tall,**" he stood tall himself, "**the Divine is in you. The alignment of your spine will bring in the Divine—always. Stand tall, sit tall, *BE* the light that you are, and whenever you doubt, stand tall.**"

Suddenly Eagle stood behind me—his wings were my wings, his carriage mine. "**You will soar high,**" the holy man said. "**It is your nature to do that. No more groveling,**" he shook his finger at me. "**That is not who you are. Fly high.**"

Now the Grandmothers appeared. "***Step into your power,***" they said, and as I stepped forward, power coursed through me. My feet and legs planted in the earth, I was so solid and rooted I couldn't have moved if I had wanted to.

When the journey was over and I was on my way back to ordinary reality a thought came that seemed so important I wrote it down. A final communication from the Grandmothers, sent to put things into perspective. "**You are not special,**" they said, "**no more than anyone is special. But you must be powerful and claim greatness as this work demands it.**"

This journey took a while for me to integrate. Like others, it too had dealt with doubt, but this time doubt was part of a cosmic condition. Unlike what I had found on other journeys, this time darkness had not been personal.

Later on while talking with Mahri, a member of the core group who had been on the spiritual path a long time, I brought up the subject of fear. "Doubt is a form of fear," she said. "I've learned that no matter how it looks, fear is always ego. This is what you're dealing with. It's actually the little self that's afraid.

"The ego tries to preserve itself; it seeks control with fear and doubt. Underneath your fear of coming out or not coming out with the Grandmothers' message is the same stuff. The ego says, you're 'not worthy,' one day and 'really hot,' the next. You get so busy worrying about being worthy or being afraid of being too self-important that you can't stay focused on what you're doing. Sneaky thing, the ego."

"Lack of confidence shows the need for verticality."

A few days later, inspired by my experience with the holy man and by Mahri's words, I journeyed to the lower world seeking strength. "I love you, Bear," I said, giving him a hug of greeting and as we embraced I thought, "Unlike Eagle, Bear is neither he nor she. Bear is simply Bear."

Bear carried me on his back. He lumbered through dense forest into a clearing where the sun shone brightly. Here stood a tall pole. Turning to me he said, **"Lack of confidence shows the need for verticality; as this pole stands, is how confidence stands."**

Races of people gathered around us and holding hands and dancing toward, then away from the pole, they called on the power of the vertical. I joined them, aware of how this dance drew the towering force of the pole into us.

"Bear," I said, "I wish to be purified to do the work of the Grandmothers, to do it with a pure and sanctified motive—purified from self-serving and purified from fear." **"Confidence and what you ask for are one and the same,"** he said as again I danced with the tribes of people round the pole.

Forming a circle that turned within a larger one, we chanted as three male dancers who looked like ancient Incans whirled in the space between the circles. Their movements were performed low to the ground but mimicked flight and all the dancers imitated them somewhat. I was one.

In my mind I saw this ritual as it had been performed in ages past, in Northern Europe as well as in the Americas. A strength bringer, it delivered power to individuals and to the nations they represented. As we danced ribbons of rain gracefully folded down, blessing and feeding those of us engaged in this work. Again I was one of many.

"This work is not special," Bear said, **"do not be awed by it. It is not special; it is only yours to do."** Reminding me that each of us has work to do, he said, **"Take an almost matter-of-fact attitude toward it. Respect, but not awe. Awe is misplaced; it feeds the ego—yours and others. It is simple. This is a time of action, a time of calling people to sisterhood and brotherhood,"** he said, and smiling at me, added, **"If you call them, they will come."**

"Give more empowerments," he said. **"Don't wait to be perfect. Don't wait to be perfect to do anything. Just do, do!"** "Okay, Bear," I nodded. He was right. If I waited until I was perfect, nothing would get done.

CHAPTER 11

Rearranging Yin and Yang

"The work you have been given is moving the energy of what you call yin so that it pushes against yang...rearranges it."

As my fear of venturing further with the Grandmothers subsided I wanted to learn more about the imbalance of yin and yang within myself and in everything. For some reason I was drawn to the lower world for this.

I dropped over the edge of my opening in the earth and dove through what seemed miles of blackness before I splashed into the river. Then climbing into the canoe I paddled until I saw the thick leaves that marked my destination. Bear was waiting on the other side of these leaves, and taking me on his back, said, **"We must travel far."**

I wrapped arms and legs around him while he lifted his nose to sniff the air before running forward. The ground was rocky but with little effort he climbed a pathway that wound upward and before I knew it we were out of the shadow of the mountain, running in the burning sun.

Bear didn't tire. The heat didn't seem to affect him as it would on earth; he wasn't even panting. I felt the sun on my arms and back but somehow it felt good. I, so prone to sunburn, was comfortable under this blazing sky. Heat waves rose from the rocks beside our path but I wasn't even sweating.

Bear pulled us up and over the top of a hill into now verdant land where a river meandered. I smelled the green of new grass and felt a breeze, but we didn't stop here. Clambering onto rock, Bear climbed until we were higher still.

Suddenly a voice said, **"Fertile and infertile, verdant and arid. These are opposites—but necessary."** The cadence was the Grandmothers', though when I looked around I didn't see them. But when I slid off Bear's back and my feet touched ground Bear disappeared.

Even the mountain was gone now and I found myself standing on a fast moving platform; I was a passenger on a flatbed that rushed through changing landscapes. Trees, mountains and gorges whizzed by me so fast I could barely see them.

Forests of conifers rolled into the distance as far as I could see. I smelled the tang of evergreens, but no sooner did I become aware of this than the forests were gone and the train sped through even higher mountains whose rocky peaks rose above the tree line. But before I could get a good look at this landscape we rushed onto a fertile plain where herds of animals were grazing.

I wanted to stop and watch them but we were traveling at such speed I could only catch a glimpse of them before I found myself in a desert where nothing at all grew, where sandy earth seemed to stretch on and on forever. Then we hurtled through another river valley and up and over another mountain.

"What is this?" I said, barely able to control my irritation. The contrasts flying before my eyes couldn't have been more dramatic yet there wasn't time to concentrate on any of them. This train was moving too fast.

Again the voice said, **"Fertile and infertile, verdant and arid. These are opposites—but necessary."** "This is what I am seeing—opposites," I said. High and low, wet and dry, hot and cold. That plunge from lushness into desert and down a rocky peak into a green valley had stunned me. The contrasts had shocked my senses.

As the voice resumed I was sure it was the Grandmothers. **"All is in change and flux,"** they said. **"What seems fertile bears within itself the seeds of its own movement into aridity. What seems arid holds the seeds of great fecundity. We dance together in an inter weaving motion."** Pausing, they added, **"What seems wrong bears within itself the seeds of right."** This was elegant language, almost poetry, but I wondered, "What does it mean?" **"Yin and yang are fluid,"** they said. **"They only seem to be opposites.**

"The work you have been given is moving the energy of what you call yin, so that it pushes against yang and *rearranges it*." This startled me. How could yin and yang, the building blocks of the universe, shift?

Reading my mind, they said, **"There is no danger for the earth or for you at this time. Neither will be destroyed by cataclysm as so many fear. There is a new movement which brings life.**

"Much of the distress and pain in the world today has to do with the stagnation of energy; energy is caught as though in little back-waters." They drew my attention to logs floating in the scum of a dead-ended stream and in the still water I saw the Grandmothers' reflections.

I looked up and was taken by their compassionate gazes as they studied this water. **"When there is no movement, no life, no growing change,"** they said, **"stagnation occurs and from this—destruction, depravation and evil. So,"** they said, **"You are a midwife, helping to give birth to the new whose time has come. This is a natural progression and growth. It is time!"** they cried, heads thrown back in triumph. **"*This* is good news."**

"How does what you are saying relate to my health?" I asked, remembering my continuing concern about my body. **"You are part of the planet,"** they said. **"Stagnation and stuck states must be moved from you as well. Your work is not separate from planetary work. What we mean,"** they added, arms opening wide, **"is there is nothing *wrong* with you! Your individual karma is being burned, that is all,"** they lifted their hands. **"The planet's karma is being burned, everyone's karma is being burned."** Smiling, they said, **"Do it with good will.**

"You are part of a process and no matter what is done this process which has begun will continue. You can be part of it. You can have the joy of being along on the ride with us and help others have that joy too, *but the process will take place no matter what you do.* Although there is nothing you need DO, for your own joy, do it! Know, however, that no one's fate rides on your actions. You are fortunate indeed to do the work if you choose, for it will give you beauty and joy." "I choose," I said, "I choose!"

Suddenly Bear, a deer and several animals began to dance around me. It was that same in and out movement that pulled old energy out. While they danced the Grandmothers spoke. **"As water in a river or stream moves, so must life move to avoid stagnation, disease and evil. Freshness, newness and clarity come with movement,"** they said. **"This change in yin and yang will bring freshness to a stagnant pond and move the fetid water out.**

"Take joy in your release," they said, **"take joy in the earth's release—great joy!"** The animals flung themselves about with abandon, overjoyed that I had been given this chance to play a part in this work and would play it with a will. As I watched I heard, **"The horrors in the world are just the cracking off of the old; stagnation is flowing off. Yin and yang shape each other by one moving against the other, each one pushing in its natural flow against the other."**

Something moved; there was a shifting of light and dark. I fixed my eyes on the moving shapes and saw...that the Grandmothers were right! The shape of yin and yang *was* changing. This wasn't the same curved, tear-shaped pattern I was accustomed to; it was morphing into different forms.

"Humans think of yin and yang only as they are drawn in their rest position," the Grandmothers said, **"when the energies achieve homeostasis for periods of time. This is the pattern you are accustomed to, your image of yin and yang. But when life begins to move this energy, to push and churn it, it makes many shapes."** They added, **Yin and yang are always of equal volume."**

When they spoke this last sentence I looked hard at them. "If yin and yang are of equal volume," I thought, "how can there be a problem of excess yang in the world?" Wordlessly they answered. The *volume* of yin and yang remains the same, but how strongly or weakly either energy manifests power can change from time to time. Yin, which has been in a depleted, dormant state for many centuries, is now awakening. This awakening yin is shifting, not in volume but in power.

Later I wondered what they had meant when they said, "Yin and yang only *seem* like opposites." As I puzzled this over it came to me that they meant yin and yang only seem like *"fixed opposites."* They are opposites all right, but fluid, *not fixed.*

"The Divine came in the form of the Grandmothers because this work is about the feminine principal, yin."

In addition to learning about the shift in yin and yang, I wanted to understand the feminine principle itself. I knew that the Grandmothers were part of this energy, but I wanted to know more about the great feminine, the yin.

When I reached their valley in the upper world, instead of landing, I kept on flying. My wings seemed to have a mind of their own today and lifted me higher. "I want to learn about the Great Mother," I repeated as I rose.

I had gone through several levels of the upper world and was wondering why I was still rising when I glanced to the side and saw Eagle. "Eagle, I'm so glad to see you," I said. "I was worrying that I had gone too far."

He motioned me onto his back, so I swung my legs over, clasped my hands around his neck and we went still higher. At last we landed and when I stepped down, I noticed that the ground was white here, as if covered by snow. In the distance snowy forms that resembled the Cliffs of Dover jutted up on the horizon.

This was a very different place, not like earth and not like any level of non-ordinary reality I had yet seen. It felt sacred. No sooner did I recognize this than a female figure with long dark hair approached. Here in this white space, she wore a light-colored robe, and about her was the aura of holiness. As I turned to examine her, I saw that she was glowing! Her face, her robes, everything about her glowed. "*This*," I whispered, "is the Great Mother." As I regarded her in awe she replied, "**People do not understand the feminine principle.**"

I nodded agreement and she said, "**The Divine has come in the form of the Grandmothers because this work is about the feminine principle, yin. It is appropriate that it would be females, the Grandmothers, who would bring this teaching. If the teaching for this time were about being a warrior,**" she laughed, "**a warrior would have come.**

"**It is time for the world to return to the nurturance, love and comfort of the Mother. Conquest and aggression have been taken as far as they can go without destroying all life,**" she said. "**Energy must now turn to supporting life—to greater compassion, greater understanding, to building wisdom rather than to accumulating knowledge.**

"**The energy of life must move,**" she said. "**There must be new goals now: life affirming, life enhancing goals that deepen the experience of being human. So that the days one lives are *good* days, *valued days*, even looked forward to.**" Gesturing outward she said, "**Looked forward to because one feels loved.**" Her arms now opened in a gesture of expansion as she cried, "**Because one *is* love!**

"**Understanding, giving, and the deepening of compassion into wisdom are qualities of the Mother. These,**" she gently smiled, "**are yin qualities. They come when one receives what the Divine is giving at all times.**

"**When the mind is busy in outward pursuit, which is yang, there can be no reception. Then there is too much busyness, too much doing and acquiring.**" Laughing, she said, "**Life is easier than this and will *be* easier as yin comes in. There will be balance then, and each will feel this balance in her and his heart, mind and body. Living will then become a pleasure, not an ordeal or a challenge!**" Her expression brightened as she said, "**Oh, there will always be challenges. That is part of the pleasure…but in balance.**"

Gazing at me with compassion, she was beauty beyond beauty; I could barely look at her. Then tears poured down my face and blinded me so I couldn't see her any more. But I could still hear her. "**Life is not** war," she proclaimed, "Life is not movement against anything. That is not life. *That* is the energy of yang—run to the end of its tether. Yang is now tired, tired," she said, "and taut."

Nodding sadly, she said, "You see one another with your distresses and problems, tensions and anguish." As her head came up, she looked directly at me and said, "We see *everything*!" The Grandmothers now flanked her, and speaking in one voice they proclaimed, "We see the energy body of the planet and the energy body of each life form. All of these are tense and pulled tight with striving, pulled tight with fear and avoidance. This must stop."

Gazing into the distance, she and the Grandmothers said, "There is great beauty in each day, there is great beauty in each being, but for *so long* humans have missed that beauty. That is coming to an end now," they said, squaring their shoulders. "This work will help it come to an end.

"Write from your heart," they chorused, "Your heart knows. We speak through your heart, we live in your heart," they said, "and hear your unspoken questions about *who* we are." This jolted me; I didn't think they knew how often I had questioned their ability to handle a task of this magnitude. Correcting the imbalance on earth had seemed to me too big a job for a group of old women. The Grandmothers and the Great Mother had me skewered me with their eyes.

"We are not separate from God," they said; "we are at one with God. God," they explained, "takes different forms at different times to give the lessons and gifts of the moment.

"We have come now." The Grandmothers spoke while the Great Mother nodded in agreement. "And our lesson for this time is the restoration of the feminine principle into correct, abiding balance with the male principle. We infuse life and energy into yin, which has become deficient and is now filling. And we take the form that would be understood to do this work. We come," they said, "as the Grandmothers, as the Great Council of the Grandmothers."

The Great Mother in the pale robe touched me on the shoulder and I bowed, but she raised me up and we gazed at one another. "We meet on a higher level of the upper world today," she said, "because here we are *far* removed from earth where there is no understanding or appreciation for the feminine aspect of God. This work," she gestured to the Grandmothers, "is bringing this consciousness into the earth in ribbons of light." Patting me reassuringly she said, "This is taking place just as it should take place."

The Grandmothers gathered around and as they came in close

they began to make me beautiful. One held up a mirror and I caught a glimpse of myself in their arms as they stroked my face and fussed over me. I looked younger.

This was strange but wonderful and as I felt beauty growing inside me they said, **"From this book will come many discussion groups and much teaching. The book,"** they illustrated with a movement of their hands, **"is a shaft of light that pierces the hard layers of the earth, imbeds itself and spreads from there. The teachings and other work that will come from this will be great."**

The drumbeat changed. As I turned to leave, my entire body was quivering, full of emotion. I was so shaky as I began my return that Eagle flew close beside me, keeping watch.

The act of worship creates a separation between worshiper and worshipped.

Because of my religious background I had imagined that the Great Mother would look like the Virgin Mary and though this Mother hadn't looked like her, she had *felt* like her. I was learning that there were many forms of the Great Mother, different forms for different cultures. This was something I had known little of, and it remained a great mystery to me.

Shortly after this journey I returned to the upper world, just to be with the Grandmothers. Wearing their human forms, they greeted and embraced me, then stepped back, and with secret smiles, looked me over. I was admiring them and feeling their love for me when out of the corner of my eye I caught movement. An enormous figure was approaching.

In glowing blues and reds, a woman who seemed to glow with light walked slowly forward. It was the Great Mother, this time appearing as the queen of heaven.

She wore a crown and looked *exactly* as I had imagined the Blessed Mother would look. As she drew near, I dropped to my knees and while my eyes fastened on the glow about her, her hands reached up and removed the crown from her head. To my horror she placed it on mine. Quickly I pushed it back to her, but **"No!"** she said, refusing it. As she replaced it on my head she said, **"I do not want your worship."** I Stared, openmouthed.

"You are to think of becoming *one* with me," she said. **"If you do this, I can begin to work *through* you. Invite me,"** she said, **"invite**

whatever form of the Divine you revere into your life. The act of worship," she explained, "**creates a separation between worshiper and worshipped. It limits the ability of the Divine to enter in and act in human lives.**

"**You must recognize your own divine nature. This is what is called for now.**" With authority she said, "*You can no longer afford the delusion that you are separate from God.* **As you begin to relate to the Divine in this new way you will help to rescue your planet.**"

No longer could I think of myself as a puny human being. I must stop living as if I were only my small self and move into the *great Self.* This was something all must do. As these thoughts came She smiled and nodded.

On my way back to ordinary reality I mulled this over. "The limitless power of Divinity wants to work in and through me, in and through each of us." I said. I vowed to stop holding myself separate from God, stop my habitual petitioning and instead turn to the stillness within. *Mergence with the Presence,* this was what the Great Mother was asking for.

"We give away, we help, offer and hold. We create a safe container for the family of life."

Several times I was asked, "Why the Grandmothers? If the energy of yin is what is needed on earth, why hasn't the Mother come? Why the Grandmothers?" This question had never bothered me as from the beginning I had loved these wise old women, so to find out, "Why the Grandmothers?" I had to journey.

As soon as I asked them, they laughed and wrapped me in a shawl. Made of soft wool, the color of earth, it framed my face, covered my back and crossed over at my breast. I looked like a Mexican grandmother wrapped in her reboso.

It was the most interesting thing. As soon as the Grandmothers wrapped me I *became* a traditional grandmother and cloaked like this I experienced life from a different viewpoint. What I noticed was, I was more an observer than a participant.

Standing in the midst of a busy marketplace, watching the activity around me, I felt somewhat distant from it. People haggled with one another and hurried by me. Men strutted, women shared stories and on the ground, children played. Hardly anyone noticed me and I simply watched. Although I had interest in and compassion for everyone in the marketplace, my consciousness was somewhat removed.

As I wondered about this the Grandmothers spoke. **"It is hard to be angry with a grandmother,"** they said, **"it is hard to even have expectations of a grandmother."** Quietly they added, **"A grandmother is somewhat removed from the drama of daily life.**

"A grandmother's position is not one of struggle," they said. **She may have sexual feelings, but she is not ruled by desire. There is not the energy of conquest and battle around a grandmother as there often is around a younger woman. A grandmother is not striving for anything. She does not demand center stage but stands back, nurtures and supports the family."** They were speaking, not of individual grandmothers, but of the archetypal grandmother. **"Yes,"** they said, and pointing to themselves, added, **"*We* do this.**

"*We* give away, we help, offer and hold. We create a safe container for the family of life. The family is safe and secure *because we are here*, because we hold and support all.

"This particular quality of the one called grandmother is something everyone understands," they said. **"Grandmothers seek the continuance of the family, they promote what is good in life; they seek to support."** Yes, I thought, it is the old ones, grandmothers and grandfathers, who hold wisdom for the human family. "This is why you have come as the Great Council of Grandmothers, isn't it?" I asked.

"This is our mission," they said. **"As the Grandmothers we hold all fathers, mothers, and children of the family of life. These are our sons, our daughters and our grandchildren.**

"We desire the highest good for all. This quality of selfless giving is what is now needed on earth. *This is why the Great Council of Grandmothers has come:* to love the fathers, to love the mothers, to love the children, to love all."

I cried as I listened. "Yes, they are the perfect fit for what the world needs now," I said. And wrapped in my reboso, I said goodbye to these loving, giving Grandmothers with only one thought in mind—I wanted to be like them.

"We will be an easy form of the Divine for people to access. We are comforting and welcoming; we are a nurturing presence."

It is these qualities of the Grandmothers that have brought people alive spiritually, filling a long-standing hunger for God.

Lorna, a member of the core group, never believed she could have a personal relationship with God until she received the Grandmothers' empowerment. An elegant eighty-year old, she said, "I struggled and searched for God for at least fifty of my eighty years." Raised a Christian, she married a Jewish man and although she put a sincere effort into embracing Christianity, then Judaism, she says "I don't know why but I just didn't feel anything inside. I tried, but religion was dry for me—it left a taste of ashes in my mouth."

Once she was empowered by the Grandmothers she kept returning, each time bringing a new friend with her to share the experience. Her eyes softened when she told us, "I never believed it could happen to me but now I have a close relationship with God. I finally have what I looked for all my life but could never find."

Sarah, who I met many years ago in a highly structured meditation class, has a similar story. Speaking of that time she said, "I followed my meditation teachers then, sticking with their strict discipline until I could no longer sustain it. I worked really hard at my spiritual life and it was so much work that after a while there wasn't any heart left in it. I finally stopped when I realized I felt no closer to God than I had when I started. I pretty much gave up on God then," she said. "I had tried as hard as I could but nothing had happened for me. I figured God must be for other people but not for me."

I lost contact with Sarah and hadn't known of the despair she had suffered so when I saw her glowing after the Grandmothers' empowerment I didn't realize how much this event had meant to her. She became part of the core group, coming to each meeting and eagerly sharing the on-going effects of the Grandmothers' empowerment. And because of her spiritual discipline, she practiced their meditations religiously and always had something interesting to share.

One day she looked at me with her dark eyes and said, "I can never thank you enough for giving God back to me. I'd lost all hope of ever having a relationship like this but since the Grandmothers, I have God back."

CHAPTER 12

The Fabric of Being

"The differences in people are only seeming differences. It is the cloak that is real."

The Grandmothers had put me through so many experiences that I now had an understanding of the Feminine Principle. Yin was no longer just a word to me; I had felt it in my body. But how could I give others this experience? This was the focus for my next journey.

Eagle flew beside me and when we reached the Grandmothers' valley I mimicked his landing, wings spread wide and feet down. I was a bald eagle with fierce face and curved beak as I bowed to the Grandmothers. "Oh, Ladies," I said, "I want to know how to help others understand the Feminine Principle." They were pleased that I was back with them, pleased also with my question.

I watched and waited, my wings folded like hands in prayer while they busied themselves with my shoulders. They were making me a cloak with a fan collar that shot from my clavicle to above my head. It was Elizabethan in style except that it stood much higher and was made not of cloth but of light.

When I returned to my question about helping others understand the Feminine Principle, I became aware of a vertical pulling. Something thrust upward through this folded collar and at the same time shot down my spine. This created a tension that held me straight; my spine was lengthening and at the same time getting hot. The center of my back was now aflame; it would have burned my fingers had I touched it.

Since I didn't understand what this was about, I asked my question again. **"You cannot help yourself without helping others,"** the Grandmothers said and I understood that through 'straightening' and making me stronger, they would also help others. "I think you have told me this before," I said. **"And we will tell you again."**

The cloak was immense. Seamless and deep blue, it appeared to be part of the night sky, the covering of the earth. **"All are contained within this cloak,"** they said. **"The differences you see in people are only seeming differences which occur on the level of life on earth."** And giving me a look, they added, **"It is the cloak that is real."**

They pointed to little bumps underneath the cloak and I watched them move around, each bump disappearing then appearing again somewhere underneath the fabric. "These bumps create a lot of activity, "I said, "but there's not much to them." The Grandmothers nodded.

It felt wonderful to be covered by this 'cloak-of-all' as they called it. Light, but comforting, it was midnight blue and covered with stars. As I studied the folds spread over me, I saw how brightly the stars glowed and recognized what it was I was looking at. "Oh," I said, "The cloak is the night sky and each being is a star in this sky!" The Grandmothers smiled broadly.

"So this is what they mean when they say, "**All are contained within this cloak,**" I thought, and then the immensity of this concept hit me. How could I teach something as grand as this? No sooner did my question form than I heard the Grandmothers say, **"Let them experience it."** I was to teach this as a meditation. **"Yes,"** they nodded. **"Let each expand into the night sky, be enfolded in the color of this sky, sense the breeze here, see and feel the starlight.**

"*This* is reality," they said. **"What you call 'reality' is not real at all."** Pointing to the cloak that covered the earth, they said, **"What you call 'real' are only the little bumps underneath the cloak, those little comings and goings beneath its folds.**

"It is the seamless fabric of the cloak that is real. This is a cloth that covers all." And folding their arms against their chests they said, **"This is the cloth of all, *the Fabric of Being! The Fabric of Being*,"** *they repeated.* **"Those who understand this teaching will be filled with joy and a sense of recognition."** Cryptically they added, **"Many will not and yet many will.**

"Not everything in this work is for everyone," they explained, **"but there is something in it for everyone."** "How wonderful, Grandmothers, that all its lessons don't have to fit in order for the Fabric of Being to benefit each person." For some time I had worried about how much of my experience with the Grandmothers I was to include in the book and what they had just said clarified this. "Put everything in," I told myself, "and let people take what they can use."

When I looked up I was surprised to see Bear with us. Thrilled to see him here in the upper world I cried, "Oh Bear, I've missed you so." His love poured out to me; I could tell that he was as happy to see me, as I was to see him.

The Grandmothers looked on as we embraced, and smiling, said, **"We joyously manifest from the Fabric of Being as a particular.... thread,"** laughing when after searching for the right word they found it in 'thread.' **In joy we manifest our particular *thread*,"** they said, **"rub against others, weave with and touch them. And by doing this, the love in the Fabric of Being is increased a thousand-fold times.**

"When we recognize one another as Bear and you just did, joy infuses the Fabric of Being. This is why everyone loves a love story. It makes us happy to see a loving act, to see a touch or look of sweetness because we *feel* it. We *feel* it in the Fabric of Being.

"Let yourselves be clothed in the Fabric of Being, and know that each one is so clothed. *Each One*." They gestured in the direction of planet Earth and said, **"Some, of course, will become fascinated by the little bumps that move around underneath this fabric, those tiny bumps that come and go."** Shrugging their shoulders as if to say, "That can't be helped," they said, **"Think of the Fabric of Being as the night sky, of yourself standing in an open place, surrounded from above, in front, behind, and at the sides by the sky. Then think of this Fabric of Being touching your skin and breathe it in."** Exhaling a satisfying sigh, they said, **"It touches all."**

I did as they directed, thought of the sky and breathed it in. There was such a feeling of peace and as I continued to breathe I felt myself expanding exponentially. "Oh—yes! Grandmothers!" I cried, lifting into euphoria.

Now I was one with the night sky, breathing it in as I sat within it, immersed in a state of expectancy. In utter happiness I rested and then, from this place of peace, I thought again of the question I had come with. How could I communicate the essence of yin to others?

Instantly the high collar of the cloak straightened above my head and a vertical tug began up and down my back. The pull elongated me and my awareness returned to my spine. I watched as the force that pulled me upward lifted the cloak too. As we lifted, I saw myself, and the cloak spread wide. I was laid open to heaven.

From a distance I peered down at my body. I, the watcher, was still myself but somehow this 'self' was now in two places. The 'me' that was lying flat was like a flower with a belled-open, cone-shaped top. I watched the energy of heaven flow into this flower, pour down my back and chest, flood and surround me and saw my body swell full of joy and expectancy. And just as the stem of a flower roots itself into the earth, so too did I. I was in full bloom, anchored in the earth.

But as my awareness merged into my flower self, I gradually became less aware of this rooting sensation and began to get dizzy. The pull down my back had stretched me to capacity and though being connected to the earth through my "stem" was helping to ground me, I was just barely able to hold the expanding energy that was flooding me. **"Take it *EASY*,"** the Grandmothers said, **"let *us* do the work."**

I hadn't realized how hard I had been concentrating. This was why I felt light-headed. I nearly laughed at myself for "trying" yet again but I was so dizzy that instead I quickly moved into a receptive state and said, "Open, I am open." Focusing on my breathing while I thought of opening, I lay, palms-up at my sides.

My mind quieted, but my back was still inflamed. I could hardly stand the heat and squirmed as I lay there. The Grandmothers said, **"Long ago, pieces of gravel got stuck underneath the Fabric of Being inside you."** An old state of consciousness was causing this burning sensation; pain had been stored in this spot a long time and was now coming to the surface.

"This is what pain is," they said. **"Once upon a time you became so fascinated by the negative circumstances and events of your life that you became unable to release them."** I peered inside myself and gasped when I saw hot stones piled one on top of another in there.

As heat waves rose from the stones I began to cough spasmodically. I couldn't stop. The Grandmothers bent over me and patiently began to separate the stones, removing the pile of hot ones from the right side of my body. I coughed the whole time they worked.

"Carrying these inside you is not only painful," they said, **"but these weights from long ago create the distraction of pain that prevents you from moving forward."**

With the holy man's help they lay me face down on a table while he cut something out of my right shoulder. After he removed whatever it was, he sewed my skin back together, and cradling my shoulder between his hands, crooned, **"slowly, slowly, slowly."** Love, like liquid salve, poured into me through his hands and when he was finished I was weak and exhausted, but at least there was no more heat in my back.

The Grandmothers looked on in compassion as they gently reminded me that this pain was a reminder of why I must work the way I do. I must get a bit of learning from them and always follow the learning with healing.

"It must go at the right pace," they said. "Please teach me this pace," I said and the word that came to me as I made my request was **"Grace. *The right pace is full of grace.* As a bird in flight, all grace,"** they said. **"Everything in its right time."** Tilting their heads, they smiled, **"The proper rhythm is never hurried. In nature there is no hurry. Plants grow,"** they crooned, **"life grows as the seasons come and go."**

Their speech hit a rhythm and I became mesmerized by it, but then they paused and seemed to ponder something. **"Oh, a plant that is forced to grow fast,"** they burst out, **"is not healthy, doesn't live long, doesn't bear well. Animals also.**

"*This is very wrong!*" they said with horror. **"This is poison, E*vil!* Hormones and chemicals to make plants and animals grow fast. Evil,"** they said, their faces grim.

"Grace," they reflected on the word. **"Each according to its own design,"** they said and added, **"Rushing human beings—this is wrong."**

The word grace connotes a natural pace, one in rhythm with the flow of life. **"Yes,"** the holy man said, **"harm cannot come if one is in the flow of life."**

"You are more than you have ever conceived.
You are as the night sky."

When this journey was over I felt as though I was recovering from surgery. For the rest of the week I was so exhausted I crawled into bed in the middle of the day. Removing those hot stones from my body had made a big difference, though. I was calmer and more peaceful.

After five days of rest I was ready to return. I now understood how meditating on the Fabric of Being would give women an understanding of the power of yin. It had certainly done that for me. But I needed a guided meditation so I could pass it on.

Before I could ask for this, the Grandmother said, **"Think of yourself as the night sky and move into its indigo blue. There are stars and there are moons here. There is a glow throughout, and *You Encompass All This.*"** This, I thought, must be the meditation.

They smiled and said, **"Move into the indigo blue sky. Now you surround everything and vibrate with life. The stars and the moon pulsate inside you just as your physical heartbeat pulses inside your body.**

"If you were not alive both within and without, you would have

no awareness of the feeling of life within you." I pondered this and they said, **"If you were only your body, if you were only your breath, or only your thoughts, you would have no recognition of any of them. But because you are much more than any of them you can become aware of each one whenever you turn your awareness there."**

They were talking about the "watcher", the soul, that part of us that observes. Nodding, they said, **"You are more than you have ever conceived. You are as the night sky. Vast."** Smiling, they added, **"You are more than this but the night sky is easy for you to grasp."** They were right. Seeing myself as the night sky gave me focus; it was easier to think of the sky than to think of being entirely formless; the image was not as overwhelming.

"Breathe in that blue," they said. **"You can do this while you look at the night sky or you can just think of this sky."** They gave me a pat of reassurance; **"This meditation will move you beyond any sense of limitation and smallness, beyond any division of 'mine, me, you,' or 'yours.' These are tiny concepts,"** they seemed to dismiss them—**"not even pin points. *You* are great!"** they said. **"You are the deep blue ever-reaching blanket of night sky. Dissolve into it,"** they said. **"Become your breath, become this deep blue.**

"This meditation will heal worry and nervousness. It will heal the body and release stress on both gross and subtle levels because it contains the truth of who you are." With serious looks, they said, **"Some will be puzzled by this meditation and some will even be frightened by it."**

Resolutely shaking their heads they said, **"That is not important. It is not important whether one does this meditation or not. It is for those who are ready for this expanded experience. Make it available to them. The cloak of the night sky covers all."** And folding their wings across their chests they pronounced, ***"You are that."***

Two weeks later I called the core group together to meditate on the Fabric of Being. The meditation was a great success and when the meeting was over we shared the sense of expansion we felt. For many this turned out to be the most meaningful exercise yet. Each one felt inside their body, the expansive, supportive nature of yin. Maria remarked that the Fabric of Being gave her greater understanding of what God is while Connie said that now she knew what the expression "we are all one" means. I felt this sense of oneness too. I was softer now, more expanded—especially in my heart.

"Spindly, spindly creation cannot hold power."

Although my back never again felt as hot as it did when the Grand-mothers removed the stones, I still had pain there. But I had learned my lesson and now followed every bit of learning from the Grandmothers with a journey for healing. I didn't need the three to one formula any more but I needed to go to the lower world for healing as often as I went to the upper world. If for any reason I forgot this, the pain in my back reminded me.

As I stood at the edge of my opening ready to dive into the lower world, I prayed for healing from the compassionate animal spirits. Then I plunged into darkness, splashed into the familiar canoe and paddled until I ran up on sand. I pushed my way through heavy leaves and almost collided with Bear who stood waiting for me.

I collapsed against his strong body and as I leaned against him I noticed my body's brittleness compared to the steadiness and strength in his. There was a quivering intensity in me that I didn't feel in him. **"I am your totem,"** he said, **"take my strength. My strength is your strength."**

I had no understanding of this selflessness and generosity; this kind of giving was beyond my experience. **"It is not selfless,"** he said, reading my mind; **"it is beyond selfless."** Seeing my look of puzzlement, he added, **"It is that all are one."**

I realized that those weren't just words to him; he knew what "all are one" meant. This was the great "give away" that Native Americans speak of, the selfless giving of good and goods for the benefit of all. "Yes, Bear," I said. "I understand and will gladly take your strength."

"The four-legged way has strength," he said. **"Walking on two legs is hard on the body. It is not natural."** Underneath his words I heard: **"Animal consciousness, the consciousness of the body, needs to be stronger in you."** Purposefully I leaned back against his chest. His strength entered through my back, moved throughout my body, and a deep steadiness filled me with power and a sense of deep-rootedness.

"I take it on; I take it in," I said as I welcomed the comforting heal-ing, but in answer he roared, **"This is not about the shedding of pain! This,"** he growled, rising on his back legs, **"is about owning and filling with power!**

"Spindly, spindly creation cannot hold power," he growled. **"Man-kind has been made spindly by too much of the mind and not enough of the heart—the instinctual knowing. Too much deference to mind. Foolish!"** he thundered. **"Wisdom and power come from the heart."**

I drank this in. **"Come here every day for healing,"** he said. My eyes widened (*every* day!), but he said, **"Just for a while. The vibration of the body will change."**

He massaged my sacral spine while the sun beat down on the backs of my legs and it felt so good. I had my butt up in the air like a dog stretching and he took a look at me and said, **"You have forgotten what you are."** I had forgotten that I had a body; I hadn't honored my body, cared for it, as I should.

I had spent so much time in my head that I desperately needed the instinctual knowing of the heart he was talking about. "I need to be in my body," I said. **"Enjoy being in the body,"** Bear chuckled. **"You *are* here. There is purpose for this body."**

Now I sat on the ground, aware of how good it was to have the earth under me, steadying and supporting. Again I asked what could be done about the pain in my back and legs, then I lay down and closed my eyes.

Immediately something shifted and I found myself sinking into the earth, so far in that when I opened my eyes, I was looking outward from the same level as the ground. "I'm not all the way under, I can still see and breathe," I reassured myself. "It's just odd—odd but not uncomfortable." Patting me, his touch reassuring, Bear said, **"Much anxiety and depression come from not being in the body enough. Too much cut off for too long,"** he growled. **"Many generations of being cut off from the earth. Not right!"** he growled, stomping a foot.

I lay in the earth and rested. "Why not?" I said. "This is non-ordinary reality, so anything goes," and after a while I noticed how good it felt to be sunk into the ground. "Yes," I said, "the earth holds and carries everything. And I am not separate from it—not separate at all."

My nose poking out of the ground, I listened to the trees around me. Murmuring and singing to one another, they encouraged me to rest. They too were sunk into the earth and through their roots drank deeply from it. **"You can too,"** they said, and sang me a lullaby. "I feel so *connected*," I whispered to the trees. "In this place there is no separation from anything." And in this ridiculous, yet now comfortable position I nodded off.

"There is no life in belief; life is only in experience."

For four days in a row I journeyed to the lower world, just as Bear had directed, and after the fourth visit I felt so much better that my mind turned from my physical pain to something the shaman had once told me. "You suffer from the great emptiness," she had said. I would go to the Grandmothers to find out what this meant.

When I asked them about the "great emptiness" they searched my face, then took my hands in theirs and stroked them. **"This was something you once feared,"** they said.

"Grandmothers, the shaman said to come to you and ask about the great emptiness," I said and no sooner were the words out of my mouth than I was sick to my stomach. Weakness, queasiness and fear flooded me.

"It was a pain you *were* in, daughter," they said. **"It is a *past* state, and there are remnants of it still."**

Fear chilled me as I stood before them. "Grandmothers," I pleaded, "please help me move through this great emptiness or else accept it. I don't want to live filled with this kind of fear."

Somehow they transported me to my seat in the council and as I looked around I noticed that by sitting together like this the Grandmothers and I formed an edifice. Our energy rose upward from the dais, converged, and closed in far above our heads. Because we sat in a semicircle the energy form we created was conical, with the narrow point at the top. As I sat, the energy from this cone began to pour downward and fill my body.

"Fear of the great emptiness was like a poison in you," they said, **"the remnants of that poison are with you still."** As they spoke fear engulfed and shook me. "Please take it," I bowed, offering the fear to them.

The fear of emptiness, of there being *nothing*," they said, **"made for a tight holding on—a holding on to roles, to people, to possessions, to everything."** "This is what I want to release," I said. **"We know,"** they replied.

Now I sat in the lotus position with my palms open while fumes rose off me forming greenish/gray smoke clouds that billowed above my head. This smoky stuff was fear, the sort of fear that makes people so unhappy they will cling to anything.

The stuff pouring off me was so strong it went far beyond the common fear of being alone. This was the fear of *nothing*; the fear that if we did not fill our lives, if WE did not fill them, there would be only emptiness. **"This fear,"** the Grandmothers said, **"comes from an orientation to yang doing instead of yin reception."** I could see this **"orientation to yang doing"** overlaying my form, creating sharp edges that stuck out at angles from my body.

"Phew!" I heard myself exclaim, as a sensation of tied-in tightness constricted my left side. Energy was bound in there and as I felt its tightness I realized I was even fearful about my husband's up-coming job decision. This was a recent issue, a relatively small concern but it too was connected to this bound in feeling. **"Foolishly fearful,"** the Grandmothers said, **"foolishly fearful."**

Staples punctured my left side and fastened into my shoulder and back, affixing the fear. But now they were loosening. The Grandmothers stood behind and above my left side, and waving a large magnet, called to the staples, commanded and pulled on them. I watched as one by one they popped off and flew to the magnet.

"Just ancient patterns of holding on," they said as they worked the magnet. Shaking their heads, they made faces to let me know that this was not difficult work. The fear was ready to move and was coming off easily.

"There is no need for you to hold on to anything now," they said; **"you are moving *past* survival; you have left survival behind."** My left side felt expanded, open.

The great emptiness had been stored in the back left quadrant of my body. The shaman must have seen it there. **"A belief,"** the Grandmothers said, **"a mass mind belief, which, due to circumstance, you also once believed."** Flashing smiles, they added, **"But not true."**

From now on I must be awake to this old belief in the emptiness of life. I willed myself to recognize it whenever it arose and not hide from it anymore. I would invite the belief in the great emptiness in whenever I became aware of it so I could see it for what it was—only a belief.

As I made my resolution I saw that the belief had a form. It looked like a desert—it was arid, sandy, and lifeless. **"The desert of belief,"** the Grandmothers said, and added, **"there is no life in belief; life is only in experience. Furthermore, when the great emptiness is not feared, it is FULL!"** They looked into my eyes and whispered, **"It is actually the great plenitude—full of spirit, full of love…"**

I could no longer hear them, and although I watched their mouths move and saw them gesture, their voices had grown dim. "Who-o-a!" I cried, as again I felt the fear trying to sneak back into me. What an eerie sensation it was to become aware of fear lurking, while I stood with the Grandmothers.

After a long pause I re-phrased my question, "Grandmothers, the great emptiness, is there more?" **"Be with us,"** they said as more quivering vibrated in my chest. Before fear could take hold of me again their great wings brushed me—front and back. Then they covered me and I lay on the ground, blanketed by their wings. "The Grandmothers are a cocoon," I said as I looked up at them, "and I'm...I'm in the cocoon." **"Which exists in the plenitude of the emptiness/fullness of life,"** they said. "Phew"! I exclaimed as I expelled air and the remaining fear from my body, and just then the drumbeat changed.

"**Stay in the cocoon,**" they said, "**stay in the cocoon.**" "I will, Grandmothers, I will" I promised as I began my descent. And then I was sliding back down to earth, inside my cocoon.

CHAPTER 13

Our Empowerment Holds Our Message Steady

"Those who receive the empowerment will embody our message for others."

The great emptiness brought up vague fears and spooky sensations that were not attached to particular memories or events. I was having nightmares but strangely, the fears that were coming up didn't feel specifically mine. Perhaps they originated in other lifetimes or in the general consciousness of the human race. I didn't know, but transformation of some kind was taking place and I had a lot to integrate inside my cocoon.

I wasn't the only one being affected by this work. Those in the core group were starting to anchor the energy of yin too. Meditating on the Fabric of Being, the Pitcher and Cup and the Net of Light was having an effect on them. They appeared stronger to me, and at the same time softer.

This work had been so helpful that I wanted to make it available to everyone. I was confused, however, about my role in passing on the Grandmothers' empowerments. How was I to reach everyone who wanted this? Perhaps there was a way to write about the empowerment that would allow people to receive it directly from the book.

When I asked the Grandmothers about this they regarded me seriously, and one seemed especially intent as she studied me. **"You write *about* the empowerment,"** she said. **"You write *about* the ritual, but reading about it is not the same as receiving it. Not everyone needs to have the empowerment,"** she said, **"but all those who want it will receive it.**

"When you write about the empowerment readers will get a description, a taste of it. That is all. But although an empowerment cannot be passed on through the written word, our message can." Seeing how intently I was listening, the Grandmothers said, **"You will be busy giving empowerments. These will help to anchor our message."**

They weren't fully answering my question, but what they were saying was important. "Okay, Grandmothers," I said, "Your empowerment is separate from the message, is this correct?" **"There is some bleed-through,"** they said. **"You will give many empowerments and those who receive them will embody the message for others. Many of those who receive it won't know it, but they are link points for the work.**

"Dear daughter," they said, **"don't worry."** They had seen my furrowed brow. **"You will give empowerments and *enough* will receive them. It is our *message* that is important. It is our *message* that is important.**

"Certain ones will take our message and do great things with it; the empowerment holds the message steady." Looking me up and down they said, **"It is because you have the empowerment that you are able to speak about our message. So take it where it is requested, wherever it is well received. We will let you know where to go.**

"There is no more to be said about this," they said. **"The empowerment cannot be passed on through the written word but our message can. Write our message and we will help you."**

"Only a certain number of people are needed to receive the empowerment and cloak of comfort in order to hold the work steady," I said. "It creates a foundation so that all can access the work. Then from your message will come new ideas that will benefit humankind. Do I have it?" I asked. **"Yes!"** twelve heads nodded. "So," I said, "the work lays down a network, a foundation upon which to build."

Forming a circle, we danced together, that in and out pattern. **"This movement strengthens the Net of Light,"** they said and I thought, "This is something the core group can do—we can dance like this to strengthen the Net of Light."

As I moved in and out with the Grandmothers I mused about the core group, which was at this time made up entirely of women. "How like women it is to give selflessly," I thought, "selfless giving is one of the most lovely qualities of women. This is what the core group has come together to do—to give.

"This is what every person who has received the Grandmothers' empowerment is doing whether they know it or not—making themselves a link point for their work, becoming part of something bigger than themselves—for the good of all. They are building a foundation that others can use and add to. Are these my ideas?" I wondered, "or is this the Grandmothers?" These thoughts continued to flow through my mind as we danced, in and out, in and out.

"Everyone who has received our empowerment needs to be thanked for the work they are doing," the Grandmothers said, "perhaps doing unbeknown to themselves. They are anchoring this teaching." They wanted me to write a letter from them, thanking each one for their participation in this work.

As they spoke I caught a glimpse of the foundation that was being built through the Grandmothers empowerments. It didn't look the way I would normally describe a foundation. Not made of cement, it was formed instead of soil, fertile soil from which every living thing could spring. Women and men who were now connected to one another through the Net of Light were building this foundation. They were constructing it. As I glanced down at my feet I saw it come together and form a rich carpet of grass.

As I studied this foundation, it reminded me of land I had seen as a child, rich Midwestern topsoil. "A solid, steady place from which to grow," the Grandmothers said, "and coming not a moment too soon." When I glanced at them in concern, they said, "It is all perfect, in God's time."

Again they reminded me that the change they had come to bring about takes place effortlessly; it happens the moment a woman accepts the caul or a man accepts the cloak of comfort and opens to receive from the Divine. "How like God," I mused, "to think of something as simple and beautiful as this. As we come to the end of the Kali Yuga, this period referred to in Vedic scripture as the Age of Destruction, the Grandmothers are laying down the fabric from which new growth can spring."

"What a gift these people are giving," the Grandmothers said, "each one drawn by God to our empowerment because of their heritage, their body type, personality, physical self, skills, gifts and weaknesses. Because of their specificity," they said, "each one anchors special qualities. She or he can therefore be the link point for others who resonate to the same. So," they said, "all sorts of people have received and will receive our empowerment.

"It is not important that they be of a certain kind—spiritual for example." For the first ceremony they had directed me to select spiritual people, but after that people just seem to show up for the event. Many who arrived were strangers to me and I soon realized I had no control over choosing who came.

"Let God pick who comes to an empowerment," they said. "Each is the link for others of their kind. This is how more are reached." This explained why all sorts of women and men had come.

"A person might seem obnoxious to you, they might seem cold, or self-effacing or some other way," they said. "But every kind of person must receive this empowerment so that all who vibrate to the same frequency that they do, receive the message through them."

Abruptly they ordered me to "Cast the nets." The Net of Light must be made available, to all. "Oh, yes," I said, "We will." Since the core group first received the Net of Light, each time we had met we had extended it to everyone.

"You will have many more journeys on our teachings," they said, "to flesh out and amplify what we have to say." As they paused, the drumbeat changed. "Grandmothers, thank you," I said, so full of respect for them that automatically I bowed and they blessed me with their hands.

A few days later I asked them to write through me, the letter to those who had received their empowerment.

They wrote, "Each of you who has received our empowerment is now part of a movement that has begun and no matter what is done by you, this movement will continue. If you choose, you can be an active part of this work. You can have the joy of being along on the ride with us and help others to have that joy too. Or you can choose not to participate. But whatever you choose, the process has begun and will continue.

"There is nothing anyone must 'do' to participate in infusing the energy of yin back into the earth. This happens automatically when a woman receives the caul and a man receives the cloak of comfort. But for those who seek active involvement with us, *do* what is given to you. If an opportunity comes to you, *take it*. Assisting others, helping us help others will give you pleasure. You can know, however, that no one's fate rides on your actions. That is already decided."

"We will give the caul, the covering, to the sincere heart, to those who are ready to receive it."

The Grandmothers had given me an understanding of the difference between their message and their empowerment, but I still wondered if there was a way people could receive the empowerment directly from them.

The moment this journey began I felt how keyed-up and nervous

I was but I didn't know why. Eagle smiled his fierce/funny smile at me as I approached him, and when I cried, "Oh, Eagle, Eagle!" he started laughing. My nervousness was obviously showing.

Off we lifted but we hadn't gone far before I heard him say, **"Let me drive!"** Like a broken record I had been asking, "Are we going through the level now? Are we going through the level?" I was being a real a backseat driver. Why so nervous?

Patiently the Grandmothers gazed at me as I said, "Grandmothers, this is really important. What do you want me to say about giving and receiving an empowerment? It's not possible for me to give everyone the empowerment and I don't want anyone to feel cheated."

I finally became aware of their silence and stopped talking when I remembered that it wasn't up to me who received the empowerment or how.

"It is *our* empowerment," they said. "*We* give it. We draw to us those who seek and are ready for this, and to such we will come. Gather, ask, and receive. We give to sincere seekers what it is they seek. We will give the caul, the covering, to the sincere heart, to those who are ready to receive it."

I felt such relief. Anyone could ask them directly for this gift. It was the sense of being responsible for passing on their empowerment that had made me so nervous. A load that was never mine dropped from my shoulders.

"Although a ceremony honors us and makes the experience stronger for you, no ceremony is necessary to receive the empowerment," they said. "It is the sincere heart that seeks to serve humanity that draws us." They repeated, "It is the sincere heart that draws us.

"Ceremony helps you recognize what you have received by stopping the incessant chatter of the mind. That is why receiving the caul and the cloak of comfort in a ceremonial way allows this gift to go deeper into the psyche, deeper into the body and mind. But we say again, it is the sincere heart that calls us to whom we will respond. Those desiring to share this experience together may devise a ceremony, but there is no one way to do this. All are welcome to this gift we give—if the desire comes from their heart.

"We will respond to the desires in the hearts of men and women," they said, "but we do not give men the same thing that we give to women. We give to men what *they* need. We are happy to give. Happy," they said as they swung their bodies from side to side, swishing their skirts like Mexican dancers.

"That is all there is to say about the empowerment. It is very simple. *We* come, *we* draw the group together, *we* know who is ready and when they are ready...." Suddenly they became blurred and indistinct and from a distance I heard them say, "We bless you. We bless you all."

CHAPTER 14

The Power of the Deep Feminine

"Love all life."

In the middle of this work with the Grandmothers my husband and I had to have two of our three pets put down. Sadie, our golden retriever had been with us for fourteen years and Willie, our orange cat, for three. Willie had come to us when he was old, with pain in his hips and back so we knew we wouldn't have him long. Still, making the final decision was wrenching.

While we were deciding what to do about him, Sadie, almost sixteen, was nearing the end of her life too. Her legs could no longer support her and we had to hold her up each time she pooped. With her thick fur, we simply couldn't keep her clean. She had been part of our lives for so long that making this decision was excruciating. Afterwards, even though we knew we had done the right thing Roger and I grieved for days.

I was haunted by images of Sadie's last minutes. When I recalled her trusting face my heart ached and I couldn't stop crying. I missed her so much I couldn't concentrate on the Grandmothers' work, and now and then I would second-guess myself, wondering if I had made the right decision. I had just lost my dearest friend and I craved to be with the animal spirits. Finally I decided to journey to the lower world to be with Bear. Perhaps my grief could be turned into something good.

As I approached my opening in the earth tears spilled down my face and heat suffused my chest. My heart was on fire. "Help me!" I cried as I plunged downward.

When I looked up Bear stood before me, expectant. "What is the most important lesson I can learn from Sadie's and Willie's deaths?" I asked.

He turned and motioned for me to follow him, but as I trailed him, I thought, "My back has been hurting so much lately, I don't know if I can walk without limping." How strange it was to have this kind of thought in non-ordinary reality. But Bear, all perceiving, picked me up and gratefully I wrapped my arms and legs around him and lay on his back. "It feels so good to have my hands in your fur," I whispered, realizing that because of him I now had an inordinate affection for bears. No longer could I visit the zoo and see them caged. All because of him.

As I rested on his warm fur I felt my love for him swell until I could hardly contain it. Quickly he glanced over his shoulder at me and said, **"Love all life."** This was a reminder, an admonishment to not make *his* form too special, but to love *all* life. I realized that his remark pertained to my attachment to Sadie and Willie.

Bear waded across a river toward a council of animals. On the bank stood an elk with a rack of antlers, a zebra, giraffe, crocodile, a variety of apes, and many others. I asked the animals about the most important thing I could learn at this time and then we studied each other.

I looked into their intelligent eyes and worried that perhaps they condemned me for putting Sadie and Willie to sleep, but no sooner did the thought come to me than they drew me into their midst. Somehow I was able to observe this scene as well as participate in it, both seeing and feeling the apes as they placed hands on my shoulders while a crocodile went to sleep, his head on my feet.

The animals pressed themselves against me and communicated their solidarity with me. I didn't understand all that was taking place, but it felt so wonderful to be included with them—they were friends to me and I to them. Our communion touched me, but I was still worried. "What about the fish?" I thought, because I still ate fish. But no sooner did this thought come to me than fish began to swim up to the bank and gathered close to where we sat. The animals and I sat at the river's edge and watched them swim back and forth before us. We were truly a family as we gathered together.

When Bear and I crossed the river I had been afraid that the animals would judge me, but now I knew they understood, sympathized and were at one with me. Grateful for their compassion, I asked them, "What is the most important lesson I can learn from Sadie's and Willie's deaths?"

The great apes held my hands while the others moved closer. I felt the warmth of their bodies and inhaled their wonderful scent, and when I looked up I saw eagles, hawks, herons and storks perched in the trees around us.

The sense of being one with them grew stronger when they said, **"Don't see the separation. See the at-one-ment."** I listened and it came to me that I *had been* at one with Sadie in the decision to put her down;

it was *she* with her love who guided me to do what needed to be done. Tears poured down my face as I recalled the days that had lead up to her death. I had prayed continuously about taking her to the vet and tried to listen to my heart, until finally I gathered the courage to do what it told me to do. We had been together in this decision.

Out of the corner of my eye, I glimpsed Willie—his thick orange coat and round head. At home with the wild creatures now he rubbed against me, letting me know he was happy, grateful that I had stopped his suffering. I was at one with Sadie, at one with Willie, with all of them. Emotion filled my chest as from inside myself I heard: **"The animals are with me and I with them."**

"In our love we offer ourselves to one another," they said, reminding me again of what Native Americans call the "give away," the generous nature of the animal kingdom. I drank in my closeness to them, and as I felt them bless me my body and mind began to resonate with the drum. Powerfully its rhythm beat away any remaining sense of separation between us and when at last it halted, then changed tempo and I ascended the tunnel to ordinary reality I was more at peace.

"Grieving is good, it deepens you and makes you one with earth."

Two days later I returned, still grieving and still fatigued. Perhaps it was because I was so tired, but as I began my descent through the tunnel I took my time and really observed it. I noticed that its walls were ridged, a vaginal tube, underlining the femininity of Mother Earth.

On the way down I called, "Bear, teach me what I most need to know. I come physically and emotionally depleted."

From a towering stance on two legs Bear reached down, lifted me onto his shoulder and carried me, patting me gently as he walked, just as he would an infant. Folded happily over him like the baby I was, I sighed. **"You are tired,"** he said, **"rest,"** and I fell asleep on his shoulder.

He laid me on the grass beside a stream, and covered me with leaves; my arms formed leaf-feathered wings. Placing more leaves over my body, he tended me carefully, especially my face and head where a headache raged. When he had entirely covered me he lifted my back a little and scooped earth and leaves into a mound beneath me. He wanted me blanketed, wrapped in the elements of earth.

"The loss of Sadie is a time for transformation and transmutation," he said, **"a special time."** Because of our long relationship, my grief for Sadie was greater than that for Willie so he spoke specifically of her. **"This brings a sacred change,"** he said, **"a time of sinking into the earth. The pull of the earth is right,"** he said and I felt this pulling; the earth was calling, drawing me to herself. **"Give in to it,"** he said, **"do not go into the mind. Slo-o-o-o-w,"** he pantomimed, **"sink in and receive."**

"Grieving is good," he said; **"it deepens you and makes you one with earth."** I followed his direction, rested in and on the earth, and when at last I opened my eyes the animals had formed a circle around us. There was reverence in this gathering, a sense of deep union. **"No animal will harm thee,"** they said, and I knew it to be true.

I wanted to prostrate myself before their love, kneel before this giving brotherhood/sisterhood, and before I could wonder where this thought had come from I was down with my face to the ground. As the animals lifted me I knew that we *were* family in the best sense of the word. There is a name for this relationship; they whispered it in my ear—an ancient name—but I couldn't retain it. No matter. We were one, secretly one—this was what it meant.

A healing was taking place within my blood that slowed and grounded me. I would need the power of my elemental nature if I was to do the Grandmothers' work; grounding and slowing down felt right.

"You must take your place in the earth," the animals said. **"Even now, even in this alien time in history, you must take your place. Claim the earth. Call on it, call on the earth."**

I did as they said while they sat with me in infinite patience, their loving care, along with the power from the earth flowing into me and sinking in. Everything shifted and settled into me until I realized that I *was* the earth, I *was* this red rock and soil. I knew this to be true but the idea was still so new to me that, overwhelmed, I began to drift off to sleep until something moved, startling me awake. Bear said, **"It's all right. What you are experiencing is a dissolution, a dismemberment."** My molecules were becoming the earth, becoming the soil on which I lay.

From somewhere above the ground I looked down at myself, but strangely I now had black hair, I was young, my body a deep brown color. It was strange because I was aware that I was in two forms at the same time; still in my usual form, I was also a dark young woman. This lithe and younger me sat cross-legged in the center of the animals, naked except for a skirt. My arms began to make dancing movements to the drum and then wheeling, they began to spin like Shiva's. I was Nataraja, the lord of the dance.

Then I stood, and lifting first one leg and then the other, felt the earth, solid and supportive beneath the soles of my feet. As I swung my right arm out, its momentum created a salute to oneness with the animals. This arm then swung the other way around the circle. The left arm repeated these movements, and then I sat, straight-backed with my palms open to receive.

"Mother Earth wants her own back," a voice said, and I replied, "I am her own. We are all her own." When I looked up I saw Bear dancing around me and with him was a wolf who approached, sniffed, then looked me in the eye. A voice said **"Sacred dog,"** his look deepened, and then he came closer and let me touch him. I clasped my arms around his neck and when I looked into his eyes I saw that I had nothing to fear from him. He was a gift; I had been given this gift of Wolf. In companionable silence we all sat together, Wolf on my left and Bear on my right. Skin to skin.

"I need this wild world!" I said, and a triumphant, "Yes!" escaped me. "How I have longed for this," I sighed, an ache in my heart. **"It is here!"** cried the animals, and as I looked to them I said, "Yes, this is the world I have longed for."

"Loving one another as Jesus said to do, this is the only act, the only action."

The next day I decided to journey to the Grandmothers and followed Eagle all the way, my wings beating in his wake. When we dropped into the valley where they stood, their wings widened in welcome. "What is your will for me, Grandmothers?" I asked as I walked toward them.

Looking up as if to say, "And what was it you wanted?" they jarred me, reminding me to be specific with my questions. "I need more guidance on your teachings," I said. I got off track with these deaths, and if I'm still off track, I want to be put back on."

Nodding, **"Yes,"** they pulled me up tall, aligned me with them. **"The deaths of Sadie and Willie have brought you into strong alignment with the animal spirits,"** they said. **"The animals are more present with you now than ever before, and more supportive. This was good—all good."** So in spite of my misgivings I was on track.

When I glanced off to the side I saw golden retrievers running. There was Sadie! Other dogs and cats were there too and there was Willie! I was so shocked by their sudden appearances that I started to cry.

"How important pets are," the Grandmothers said, **"they link us**

to earth, feed and rest our hearts." Horses were present too, reptiles, fish and all kinds of plants. **"Nurture something, that it may nurture you,"** the Grandmothers said. **"The love and nurture given to a living thing is worship. Such acts reclaim the sacredness of the earth.**

"Caring for plants and pets are easy ways to connect with the sacredness of earth. These things can be done every day no matter where you are. Acts like these reanimate the energy of the sacred, bring it back to life." They paused to let me assimilate what they had said, and then cried, **"Awaken the sacred connection!**

"Wherever there is nurturance of one of the kingdoms of life, there is a sacred place. Much good comes of these sacred places— goldfish bowls, ferns, potted plants. Each of these feeds the sacredness of earth that has been smothered for so long. Do this," they said, **"with reverence; it is a bit of the source of life you hold in your hands. With this thought in mind, you will do great good. This,"** they said, **"is what holds the world together, what turns the path to love and light. Say this,"** they said.

"Look at life as it *does* occur," they said. **"Look at each tree as it *does* exist and give thanks and loving communication to it."** Pointing at me, they said, **"You have mourned so for the passing of the trees, for the passing of the land and of the animals. *Now* put your emphasis on the sacred presence of those who remain. Every plant, no matter how tiny, is sacred. Each African violet is sacred.**

"Recognize the presence of the divine life *everywhere*. It *is* present." With rueful expressions they shook their heads. **"Much damage has been done, yes, but the divine life is still present. Love it, and good will multiply from this love.**

"No act of love is small. A smile to a child, a smile to a stranger— these are great acts. Touching another in compassion is a great act. There is no order in miracles," they quoted from *A Course in Miracles*. No act of goodness is greater or lesser than any other. **"The great act is the loving heart in action. Recognize this. These acts are all around you.**

"Greet the love inside each heart," they said, **"and don't be distracted by the hurry, worry or anger you may see in another. These are only outer manifestations of a temporary imbalance."** Gently they said, **"There is love inside each one. Greet that.**

"Such acts weave stronger the Net of Light and Love throughout the earth, throughout all the universe." They paused, **"There are no great acts. We mean there are no acts greater than these. The expression of**

the loving heart is *the great act.* Nurture this greatness within yourself from moment to moment, and to your own dear self, express this love.

"Loving one another, as Jesus said to do, is the only act, the only action. Everything else is reaction. *This is the action,*" they repeated, "*loving one another!* Love each plant, love the breeze, love the smile on another's face, love the care she carries on her back. Loving, loving," they mused, "this is the great acceptance, the great embrace of the Mother. Loving in life, loving in birth, loving in death. Accepting and giving love," they said. "Great understanding comes from this, but first there must be the will to love, no matter what."

When it was time to leave them, it was especially hard for me tear myself away. Understanding my reluctance, they pressed my hands in blessing and I knew without a doubt that I carried their presence with me. They had talked about the sacredness of life, of loving what *is,* not in dwelling in grief for what is not. This was what I wanted to do.

CHAPTER 15

Men's Role

"Women have not had something of their own. This is your own."

For several months women had asked me, "What about men? What part will they play in this work?" But when I finally took this question to the Grandmothers they said nothing to me, but instead turned to each other in light-hearted laughter.

I noticed that they were dressed in silky gowns of varying pinks, and as they sat together, some of them reclined on lounging couches. They had never appeared to me like this. They looked like movie stars and society ladies from the 1930s! The scene reminded me of an old cover of *Vogue*, with the Grandmothers the essence of femininity and sophistication. Finally I took my eyes of them, and looked down at myself. I too was wearing a gown, a dusty pink color.

The Grandmothers giggled together and like young women, occasionally burst into peals of laughter. One of them with dark curly hair was especially lively—she reminded me of my mother in her youth. I was determined to stick to my question though, not be distracted by their appearance, so again I asked about the role of men in this work. And no sooner were the words out of my mouth than I noticed that off to the side of the Grandmothers stood a form, straighter and stiffer than theirs. Not at all relaxed or flowing, this form was rectangular in shape—rather like a stout column. As I waited and watched, the Grandmothers said, **"Only a few men will have a role in this work.**

"Many men will be sympathetic to our work and will understand it," they said. **"Some will dismiss it, but then there will be women who will also dismiss it."** Their expressions seemed to say, 'Well, what do you expect?' **"A few men will have a role in working with the energy of yin,"** they said, **"some already do. To these men we will gladly give the cloak of comfort."**

"Grandmothers, are the empowerments ever to be given to men?"

I asked. "Women worry that men are being left out; they don't want to be sexist." Since I didn't know what else to say, I stopped speaking and when I brought my eyes back to them I was surprised to see a great tree. I watched its roots and branches spreading far and wide and wondered why the Grandmothers were showing me this.

Realizing they would tell me about it when they were ready, I went back to my question, "Is there anything you want me to say about the role of men in your work?" "**This work is about receiving, it is about being receptive,**" they said. "**All need to receive, men and women, plants and animals. Male Native American teachers know this, men who teach Buddhism, eastern thought and meditation know this, and these men will help others.**

"**Men don't need our empowerment,**" they said, "**they need the cloak of comfort. Masculine power is of another kind. Male power is equally valid, it is very good, but it is of another kind. It is women who have not known power. Our empowerment would not help men.**"

As they spoke for some reason I found myself thinking of my son and then I saw him standing in a clearing in a forest. Power from the Grandmothers, like a strong wind, bent trees as it rushed though the forest but when it came to the clearing it bypassed my son. I watched it glance off his body and travel on.

"Why did that that power pass him by?" I wondered. "**The power of masculine energy is different from what we offer,**" they said. "**We comfort and steady men, but masculine power is not what this work is about; there is other work coming in for men—important work, but not this work.**

"**The energies of masculine and feminine must be respected for their differences. They are designed to be different. This is their purpose. All are *not* the same nor should they be,**" they said. "**This work is *specific*. Although it is primarily for women, *all will benefit* from it.**

"**There is a desire of many to equalize, to have, as you say, a level playing field. *That* is not what this work is about. The energy of yin goes deep; it is for women and goes deeply into them. This work is not about creating a falsely democratic arena, it is about embodying yin—*deeply*.**"

"Is there anything else you want me to pass on to others?" I asked as I watched their faces. "**Our empowerment makes a woman more deeply, more truly feminine,**" they said, "**and this would not do for men.**" They burst into laughter at the thought and I joined them.

"A misunderstanding of power lies behind your question," they said. "It is the yang concept of 'power over' and power 'in order to' that is behind your question. Yin is not like that. Yin is the power of the deeply feminine. It is soft and hard at the same time. It is difficult to describe."

I looked at them as they sat before me, so graceful and lovely, and said, "That's why you're dressed the way you are today—beautiful, feminine and flowing!" They nodded, "Yes." "And that's why you showed me that form, the one that looked like a squared off column. That was male energy, wasn't it? That's why it looked so different from you."

Smiling, they began to fuss over me, straightening my gown and my hair. They were elegant mother hens, so proud of their chick. Then they rose from their seats and began to dance, first with one other and then with that upright, rectangular form of yang.

Their energy was curving and fluid; like flowing water it rolled over and around the energy of yang. Swooping and circling, it appeared to fold in on itself as it curled over the stiff form of yang. In constant motion, the Grandmothers swooped back and forth, creating different patterns and rhythms. "Grandmothers," I said, "I see now how wrong it would be to give this power of yin to men."

Masculine energy is more fixed than fluid. I watched as it advanced and saw that it was more static in its motion, more concentrated. It had a forceful quality; yang was thicker and more compact. It moved less frequently than yin, but when it did, it moved quickly and with thrust. Yin swelled and flowed in all directions simultaneously but at any moment yang traveled only one way, thrusting up/down or forward/back, in one direction at a time.

The movement of yang followed its rectangular form; energy flowed along the length of it. The Grandmothers showed me the rectangle as it lay on its side and I watched its energy travel along the ground. When they stood it on end the energy moved in an up or down direction.

"What an enormous difference there is between yin and yang," I said. "It would be unseemly to infuse the power of yin into men. They would become disoriented and wouldn't know who or what they were." Smiling at me the Grandmothers said, "Yin is of the deep feminine."

Women ask about men and the empowerment because we don't understand the difference between these energies. "Grandmothers," I said, "help me to understand this so I can help others too." "Women have not had something of their own," they replied, but this is your own. It can be no other way."

Laughing they said, "Do not worry about men now. First take on and master yin; take it in, live with it and learn its ways." They smiled and said, "Then notice the effect this energy has on men; notice how it helps them. Once you have owned and anchored this power," they said, "*all* will receive comfort by your very presence."

As we held hands, I was again taken by how beautiful we were. "Is there more I should understand in order to pass this on?" I asked. "We think you understand pretty well," they said as the drumbeat changed.

As I began my descent from the upper world, I said, "The work of the empowerment is not for men. It deepens the feminine and it is not for men to be deeply feminine. It is for them to be deeply masculine. But this work gives them an appreciation of the feminine." I wanted to know more.

After this journey I caught myself looking at my husband and son with new eyes. I was curious. I wanted to understand yang energy and to do it I knew I had to get beyond my stereotypes of "male behavior." What the Grandmothers had said seemed to especially apply to my husband. In most situations he *does* move in one way, and moves with great force. I had never understood this tendency in him and had sometimes thought of it as "controlling." Now I saw it as nothing more than the nature of yang asserting itself.

"This is male energy. Hard and sharp as the intellect is sharp, or as a weapon is sharp."

When I next returned to the Grandmothers they stood as bald eagles with black and white feathers in strong contrast. I greeted them and asked for more understanding of the difference between yin and yang. When they did not move or speak, but stared at me with their fierce eagle faces, they made me aware of the serious nature of my question. The starkly contrasting feathers also told me they had anticipated it. "Yes," they said. "The white and black. Yin and yang are shown like this."

One of them pointed, and as she gestured with her hand/wing I saw that off in the distance spiky objects were sticking out of the ground. They looked like cartoon mountains—too narrowly pointed to be real. "This is male energy," the Grandmothers said. "Hard and sharp as the intellect is sharp, as a weapon is sharp. It is forceful, thrusting ... aggressive. This," they said, "is the power needed for building, for change, for combat and war."

The Grandmothers showed me an open plain. I watched men gather there and noticed that as they came together they wrestled, joked, and pummeled one another in play. Some milled about aimlessly, while others lifted heavy objects, tested their prowess on one another or competed in every conceivable way. A few of them stood quietly.

I saw warriors and conquerors; some of them wore suits and some wore armor. Men acquired objects or money; some built things, while a few attacked animals or people. And, strange as it seems, all of these activities, even the hostile ones, were performed in a matter-of-fact, almost playful manner. Yang energy had a boyish, youthful quality to it, and as I watched I heard myself say, "This is the energy that runs our world."

No sooner were the words out of my mouth than the scene changed and before me stood a forest. Stands of redwood and pine covered valleys and hills, lining the mountains that stretched into the distance. "Oh!" I cried, as the Grandmothers showed me how the energy of yang wanted to cut these forests down and as I watched, the trees began to fall.

"Yang wants to build, to dig, delve and acquire; this is its nature. It does not value trees for themselves, but views them as resources to be used for something else. Yang always asks the question, 'What are these good for?'" Forests stand for future buildings, lumber and wealth.

"Yin is different," the Grandmothers said. **"Yin is the earth *under* and *within* the forest, it is the richness from which the forest springs. Yin doesn't build things; it grows them. It is the fertile place where everything grows. Yin is not about *doing,* because it is not its nature to do.**

"The infusion of yin on the planet must start with women," they said. **"After all, it is women who grow and carry a child inside their bodies. This is patient work; this is yin. There is no *doing* necessary with the energy of yin because most things grow without intervention."** Once the seed is planted, growth proceeds on its own.

"Yang is good for change; it is needed to *make* change. It manufactures change and moves energy in a new direction." This explained the spiky "mountains" the Grandmothers had shown me at the beginning of this journey. These had not been natural growths; instead yang had moved energy in a different, and to my eye, odd direction. **"There is excitement and nervous energy in yang—a high energy,"** the Grandmothers said.

"Yin is more relaxed, yin is—is," they said, and I felt this quality of "is-ness" as my body expanded, spread deep and wide, and encompassed everything. Whatever "I" was at this moment was enormous and founded deeply in the earth. **"Yin is holding and fertile,"** the Grandmothers said; **"yin goes on and on."** A sensation of ease and connectedness filled me, a peace that would never end.

"Yang has a tendency to flash out and up," they said, **"its energy is active,"** and inside me I heard and felt "buzz, blitz, and zip." What a shock, after the steady influx of yin. These two couldn't have felt more different.

As the strident energy of yang built inside I told myself, "This is as it should be, we need both energies for a richer world." But as yang swelled, I no longer felt so philosophical. The Grandmothers were giving me a taste of yang as it is today—wild and out of control. "It's boiling!" I heard myself cry, "It's coming on so fast." My body was shaking, almost convulsing with run-away energy; I could hardly bear the tension inside me. Terrified, I cried, "There's no rest in this! Grandmothers, help!"

Once again the peace of yin descended and as my body stopped quaking I sobbed in relief. **"Yang needs yin for peace,"** they said. **"It needs a place to rest. And Yin needs yang when it wants change."**

Yang couldn't control itself. It was as helpless as I had been. I would never have been able to bring myself into balance again without the intervention of yin. I looked up to see the Grandmothers smiling, happy that I understood. **"The world has been yang for so long that it needs to be yin for a while,"** they said. **"Everything is tired and needs the rest of yin."**

"Those caught in the coils of yang the way I was just now don't realize how exhausted they are," I said. "They live in a frenzy of activity, rushing from hit to hit—from man to woman, from project to project. No rest, no peace."

The Grandmothers looked on patiently, and though I was aware that they knew this, it must have been the left over energy of yang that kept me talking. "There isn't the ebb and flow from action to rest, the flow from reach to withdraw, or from go to wait. The natural rest period in life is now *resented!*" I said with dramatic effect. "People don't want to rest. They want more *go*, more *reach*, more *strive!*" I looked up to see their patient smiles, and my demonstration of excessive yang finished, we had a good laugh together.

"Yang with no yin to hold it or lean against makes men hard and cut off"

What had the Grandmothers meant when they said, **"Women suffer from impotence while men suffer from tyranny and deprivation,"** or was it depravation? They had made this statement over a year ago and though I wasn't sure which they had meant, I had never asked about it.

Dressed in ball gowns with full, full skirts, they gazed at me with smiles of gentle understanding while light flashed from the jewels they wore in their hair. I was again enthralled by their beauty, but equally determined not to let it distract me. "Grandmothers," I said, "you told me that due to yin-yang imbalance man suffers from tyranny and...I wasn't sure if you said depravation or deprivation. Which was it?"

"It is deprivation they suffer from," they said. **"Men are not full, but empty and hollow. This is a painful state for them,"** they shook their heads in sympathy, **"and they try to fill this emptiness. Some seek women to fill it, some seek activity, and some seek alcohol or drugs.**

"When life is in balance men are filled with yang, and filled to a lesser degree with yin. Men are also supported by yin," they said, and explained, **"yang rests in, leans on and is supported by yin just as yin is supported by yang. But when both the inner and outer support of yin is absent, men are left empty. Yang, with no yin to hold it or lean against makes men hard and cut off."** Shaking their heads they said, **"Men are then cut off from their feelings, from women and from themselves.**

"Do not waste your time trying to understand why men and women are the way they are now," they said. **"If you try to make sense of this all you will see is a distortion of the relationship between male and female. Twisted and mixed up,"** they said in disgust. **"Why study that? Correct the state—do not study or bemoan it.**

"As a woman fills with the energy of yin she affects all life around her. *Everything* **benefits from a woman who holds this energy. As you fill with yin you will feel good and you will see the effect you have on those in your lives.** *Everything*," they said: **"men, animals, plants and rocks will resonate and respond to you. All life needs this energy of nurturance and support."** Looking hard at me they said, **"***You* **need it!**

"Let yourself experience this in-filling; ask for the energy of yin to fill you. Seeking this for yourself is not a selfish act. This act blesses you and blesses all life. This," they said, **"is grace.**

"Opening to yin is the most important thing a woman can do." With serious faces they said, **"Men cannot do this; they cannot help themselves receive this energy they so desperately need. But as you**

open to the Feminine Principle, men will automatically find relief." Gazing into my eyes they said, **"For the good of everything that lives, we urge you to do this."**

"Yes!" I said, again committing myself to this work, to the Grandmothers who surrounded me. They moved toward me and I felt the warmth of their skin and the silkiness of their gowns as they covered me in pinks and mauves. I was wrapped and warm, safe and happy. Such peace. And they were happy too; I could feel the vibration of their happiness humming inside me. "Um-m-m, u-m-m" it sounded, on and on.

Happy and feeling complete, I turned to say good-bye to them, but they spoke again. **"Some may think our message harkens back to an old-fashioned, limited view of women,"** they said, as a picture of subdued women and angry men flashed in my mind. **"This is not true,"** the Grandmothers said, shaking their heads. **"Yin fills a woman with power. It does not limit her.**

"Both women as well as men carry the energy of yang, so however a woman is drawn to use yang energy in the world, she will. Each person is different and some women carry more yang within them than do others just as some men carry more yin.

"There will be women who will be leaders in every field of life. Yin gives them a foundation for this; it gives everyone and everything a foundation. After a woman fills with the energy of yin she will become more effective in the world."

Stepping back, they showed me what happens as yin and yang come into balance. First I saw masculine energy as it is today, one-sided, so out of balance that it caused men to list in one direction as they walked. These men were ready to topple over. As they received the balancing energy of yin their form filled out. I noticed that this differed from man to man; some filled more on the previously empty side while some filled right down the middle of their bodies. The effect, however, was the same; they became balanced.

The process was different with women. I watched the energy of yin enter through the center of a woman's skull, spread downward and outward from there, and finally taper to a point at her feet. As the energy entered her body, it shaped itself into a sword of light.

Next the Grandmothers showed me what the energy of yang supported by yin looked like. Though slightly rounded at the tip, yang still thrust outward, although yang in balance with yin looked like more natural—like a pointing finger, an erect penis or a drop ready to separate from a body of water. **"Yang, held and reinforced by yin, will always reach out in support of life,"** they said.

The Grandmothers and I stood shoulder-to-shoulder and leaning into each other, shared our happiness at the balanced forms of female and male. Smiling, they then turned to me and showed me myself. I looked into the mirror they held before me and saw that I was wearing a gown like theirs and there were jewels in my hair too.

"Yin/yang imbalance has created depression and simmering anger in women, anger and desperation in men."

The next day I went back. "What has the over emphasis on yang energy done to men?" I asked. **"It has made them brittle,"** the Grandmothers said, **"pulled them taut and far from their own center of being. This has made them harsh with themselves and with others, quick to act and quick to lose their inner balance.**

"The overemphasis on yang has made men too dependent upon the women in their lives. This is where they get sustenance; women are the only ones they can turn to for support and love." With looks of pity they said, **"The reliance on females for 'inner food' has made men resentful of women."** Again they folded their arms for emphasis.

"Men want to be self reliant but because they are pulled so tight, they cannot emotionally support and rely on themselves." They showed me a tightly strung wire, stretched to the sky. I watched men struggle to stand, trying to mimic the wire, but the stretch was too extreme for them, causing so much strain that many of them fell over.

"Men are frustrated," the Grandmothers said. **"They do not feel good and often act out in violence, in addictions, in abuse of women, children and of society. Because of the severity of the yin-yang imbalance men are running amok."** They looked sad as they said, **"Men are more desperate than are women for a balance of yin and yang. The yin/yang imbalance has created depression and anger in women and anger and desperation in men."** Towering to an enormous height they cried, **"Enough!"**

On the way back to ordinary reality my heart hurt and my throat was tight. I ached for both sexes, but now, most of all for men.

"There is a good deal of anger now between men and women."

Several days later I returned, asking, "Is there more you want to say about yin and yang?" **"There is a good deal of anger between men**

and women," they said, "a misunderstanding of one another, a misunderstanding of self. There is a great deal of resentment—the battle
of the sexes," they said. "When women ask 'What about men?' they
are afraid that feminine power will not be sufficient to balance and
correct the excesses of yang energy."

As they spoke I noticed that I was growing larger and larger, like a
tank filling up. "This is the yin reservoir," they said. This reservoir was
a result of their empowerment; it enabled me to fill with and store yin.

I took in a breath as I swelled to an even greater size, and as I slowly
exhaled they said, "The empowerment brings woman into a vertical
position." I stood before them, amazed at how tall and full the empowerment had made me. I was so much more than I had been before.

"Women feel they are no match for men in aggression, in hardness and in that acquisitiveness of yang energy," I said. "Grandmothers,
please tell me about that."

They didn't speak, but turned away to regard the growing tree they
had showed me earlier. "Oh!" I said. "I see what this tree is!" When we
look at a tree we see only the outer tree—its branches and trunk. We
don't see the inner tree—its roots and supply system. But without the
supply system and the grounding of its roots there would be no living
tree. Viewed as a whole, the tree demonstrated the balance of yin and
yang.

"Women will not work against men," the Grandmothers said,
enunciating carefully so could I hear how ridiculous this idea sounded.
"Women fear that as they fill with yin they will work against men;
that yin and yang stand in opposition to one another," they shook
their heads in disbelief. "Some have come to consider even the relationship between yin and yang a power struggle.

"No, no," they stated. "As women become stronger, the tree is
stronger. The roots of the tree are able to draw more, so the tree itself
is greater. The whole tree is healthy. Strong women, not aggressive
women, but strong as the tree is strong. And from this," they said, "a
strong world, a strong society.

"You see things in opposition to one another," they said. "Humans
are habituated to this either/or thinking. That is yang!" they cried,
"that is yang. *That* is not the *whole* truth.

"It is very hard for you to understand this," they said, observing
my struggle to comprehend their words. "Feel the truth of this inside
yourself," they said. "Feel your own roots, feel your deep connection
to the earth.

"**Now think of the tree that stands before you,**" they said, "**and become one with it.**" As I followed their directions, my breathing slowed and deepened. I was shifting into a state of oneness with the tree and now I could feel its roots, branches and its network of supply running through me. I was massive, grounded, immovable. "**Do this at the next meeting,**" they said. "**Explore the roots of your tree.**"

Merged in the tree, I rested, and when I looked upward I saw Mother Earth. Gracefully she skipped between the branches of the tree, underneath the roots and right up through the trunk.... The last thing I remember before dropping into sleep was the fairy-like trail of her gown as she climbed in through the trunk.

I wakened as the Grandmothers said, "**Roots must be established.**" The roots of the tree fanned out in every direction, creating a grid of support. "This is another way of seeing the Net of Light," I thought as I watched how the roots wove throughout the earth, connecting everything. "**These roots are people in their power,**" the Grandmothers said. "**Roots and people touch one another and hold the earth steady.**" Rooted as I was, I felt as well as heard what they were saying.

"**This is enough about men,**" they said, folding their arms. "**Men and women do this exercise with the Tree. It will open them to receive from the Great Mother; it will help them open to the energy of yin within themselves. This exercise is for everyone.**"

The experience with the tree reminded me of an exercise in *Cutting the Ties that Bind,* by Phyllis Krystal. In her work the tree is a symbol for security and connection between heaven and earth. As I recalled this I again sensed the roots of the tree and became aware of my connection to it and to everything. "**You, especially need to feel this,**" the Grandmothers said. "**Earthed and anchored you must be.**" I knew what they meant. I had dwelled too long in my mind. I needed to be rooted.

On the way back to ordinary reality I reviewed, "The inner workings of the tree are yin, without which every tree in the world would die. We must nurture our trees, especially our inner tree, because these roots are like the Net of Light. They connect us and hold the earth together."

Cutting the Ties that Bind, Phyllis Krystal, 1993, pub. Samuel Weiser. A collection of spiritual tools for transformation and connection to Divinity, techniques for freeing oneself from the constraints of the mind, society, family and the past.

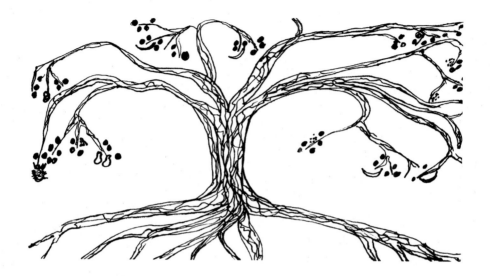

CHAPTER 16

The Tree of Life

"This place, the garden, the house and surroundings are building power."

After the journey on the Tree I didn't return to the Grandmothers for nearly two weeks. For some reason I found myself again filled with anxiety and depression, feeling edgy and isolated. This finally became so uncomfortable I could hardly stand to be inside my own skin. "What is this awful feeling?" I asked, "What is wrong with me?"

As I began my journey I had no energy of my own and was able to make the transition to non-ordinary reality only by grace. But Eagle was waiting for me at the first level of the upper world and I felt so weak that instead of flying on my own, I lay down on hi back. Because of the state I was in, everything was vague and cloudy, but when at last I peered over his shoulder I saw the Grandmothers waiting in the valley below us.

"Oh, Grandmothers, help," I pleaded as I dropped before them. Their comforting wings closed round me and once again they created a cocoon and swung me back and forth inside it, looking me over with their eagle eyes.

"Please see everything, Grandmothers," I said as they studied me. "In the past two weeks I've grown so depressed I haven't been able to journey at all. I don't know why, and my mind is just full of itself." As I said this I noticed that the holy man was there too, standing behind them.

They enclosed me in their circle and one of them reached in and extracted something from my middle. I watched as she pulled out a black, insect-like thing whose barbed pincers had been stabbing at me. This crawly thing had created my depression; it had made everything in me hurt and feel somehow wrong.

They ran piercing eyes down the back and front of me. "Oh, yes," I said, wanting them to see everything. When they pulled something else out of my stomach, I heard a sound like "pow!" as air whooshed from my lungs and another black thing exploded out of me. Now I started to shake; my body cold, as if in shock, and for a minute or more the only sound I could hear was my own ragged breathing. Then my breath grew calm and I heard myself say, "The Grandmothers are breathing power into me."

Standing behind me was the massive tree they had shown me earlier, the one whose roots had spread so far and deep. For some reason I said, "Grandmothers, help the tree too."

They made no answer but instead their hands plunged in through my spine and I sobbed as again they penetrated my body and pulled more out of me. I watched them fling dark objects into the air and began to really cry, more from shock than pain.

This stuff, the cause of my misery, had been so well hidden; I hadn't known it was there. My training as a therapist had taught me to believe that the pain of unresolved issues from childhood is what causes most depression and anxiety. But the black things the Grandmothers were pulling out of me went way beyond this explanation. I had no understanding of this stuff; it was primitive, primordial.

They waved hands over my back to seal my spine, and although I was still weak I could sit up, but just barely. **"That's enough for now,"** they said as they propped me from behind. **"You needn't understand all that we are doing or all that we will do in the future,"** they said. I was not to bother with the whys and wherefores of those nasty black things. **"This is enough for now,"** they said, **"this is just garbage from**

the past." From this I understood that the black things I had seen originated in lifetimes long, long ago.

"You must be strengthened," they said. **"Your aura, your bones,
vertebrae, digestion and breathing. Let the power of the garden
heal and fill you. It will strengthen you."** I was so grateful to them for
removing this awful stuff from me, but as I attempted to stand to thank
them, my knees buckled. I would need time to heal from the work they
had performed.

"You are our vessel, we will help you," they said, and showed me
myself seated on a bench in my garden. **"This place, the garden, the
house and surroundings, is building power. Let it fill, guard and support you. Commune with it. Go into the garden and be at one with
it."**

I thought I had known how valuable my home was to me, but from
what they were saying it was important in a way I had never considered.
Again I saw the eagle that had landed in the garden. The vortex or power
center of the Grandmothers was directly aligned over the power center
of my home. **"Be aware of this alignment,"** they said, **"and each time
you come home, step into the vortex."**

As I thought of the people who were coming for an empowerment
the next Saturday, they said, **"It will be according to our will. All will
be according to our will. No hurry. No worry. No waste."**

Now I noticed that the Grandmothers and I were inside a vortex.
"This, they said, **"makes a safe place for us to work on you."** As I stood
with them, I looked down at my body, which I saw lying on my bedroom floor. This was where I always positioned myself for a journey
but as I observed myself, I saw that *the Grandmothers were in the room
with me.* "Where am I?" I asked myself. "Am I in ordinary reality or in
the upper world? How can I be in two places at the same time?" The
Grandmothers were so *present* that I wasn't sure which reality I was in.
Finally I stopped trying to figure it out and went to sleep.

After this session I spent the whole day in the garden and by evening
my anxiety and depression were gone.

*"The problem with life today is …that the tree has not been seen
as a unit."*

If simply spending time in my garden could do so much to heal me,
what could working with the great Tree do for me and for everyone? I
wondered if the tree they had shown me was the archetypal Tree of Life.

135

When they had spoken of it that had said, **"The Tree embodies both the masculine and feminine principles of life."**

"Yes, this is the Tree of Life," they said as they pointed to its laden branches. **"It is a heavy bearing tree."** Today it looked like a child's drawing, with an over-sized canopy and lots of shiny red apples. But when I looked more closely I saw guavas, oranges, pineapples, bananas, and fruit of every kind hanging there.

"Each can pick a fruit," they said, **"the fruit is theirs to hold and savor."** I saw people from the core group walking toward the tree, each returning with a fruit. **"The fruit you receive from the Tree gives your life its savor. It is specially chosen for you,"** the Grandmothers said. Each person was given a fruit; they didn't choose it. The fruit represented the life they had been given—their gifts, their challenges, and the circumstances of their birth. The Tree of Life gave them these, the Tree, symbol for the Source.

"In nature there are no duplicates," the Grandmothers said. **"There may be similarities, but each fruit is unique. Savor, smell, touch, taste and then merge with your own fruit. Learn its particular qualities,"** they said. They wanted us to honor all the gifts, challenges and circumstances of our lives for everything that comes to us has purpose.

"The Tree bears for everyone," they said. **"It bears (produces) and bears (carries and upholds.) There can be no separation from this Tree, unless one chooses to separate oneself from it. And even this separation is false,"** they said, **"as life must finally return to the Tree."** They were showing me the cycle of life.

"You nourish the Tree of Life by giving to one another and by living out the cycle of your lives." As they spoke, the Buddhist monk Tich Nhat Han's words come to my mind, "When the flower is on its way to the garbage, the garbage is on its way to the flower." Nothing is lost in the cycle of life. A wilted flower simply becomes compost to feed the next flower; everything feeds and is fed by the Tree of Life.

"You are given fruit—your life," they said, **"and by honoring your life, you too bloom and bear fruit."** "Fruit" includes not only what we are given at birth, but also what we produce from what we've been given.

"There is a cycle," they said. **"First,"** they held up a finger, **"lean on the Tree and let it bear your burdens. Next, allow the Tree to give you your fruit. By accepting it, you too will become able to give. As you digest the fruit from the Tree of Life you eventually *become* one with the Tree."** "We give back, and the life cycle of the Tree continues. Grandmothers," I said, "this is too much for my mind." **"We Know,"** they replied.

"You need to know the Tree as a whole," they said. "It is one; roots and branches are one. The problem with life today is not only that the roots of the Tree, the feminine aspect of the Divine, have been neglected," they said, "although they have been. The problem is that the Tree has not been seen as a unit.

"Breathe now from the roots of the Tree," they said, "drawing energy up as you inhale. Do this three times. Then breathe from the branches of the Tree and draw energy down into your body as you inhale. Do this three times also. Your exhalation need not be directed anywhere," they explained, "it will go to where it is needed. But drawing the breath both up and down into your body is important."

"Show me, Grandmothers," I said, and followed them, drawing breath first from the yin of the roots and then from the yang of the branches. When I exhaled I thought of my out-breath as a blessing, going to wherever it was needed.

"Both men and women can do this exercise," they said. "If all the branches of the Tree were cut, the Tree would die; if all the roots were cut, the Tree would die." This exercise would work to harmonize yin and yang.

"There is too much fighting between the sexes now, too much 'better than/worse than,'" they said. They were talking about power struggles between men and women. "Yes," they nodded, "don't waste time on that. None!"

With urgency they turned and faced me. "The Tree needs attention and care. The *whole* Tree needs care," they said. "Just as women need care, the dear men need care."

"As you breathe from the roots and branches of the Tree, both earth and sky, yin and yang come together in an embrace. This exercise fosters love."

Standing in a circle with their arms lifted skyward, they reminded me of Native Americans as they intoned, "To all my relations. All! All are in union with the Tree of Life." When they turned back to me, they said, "There is a realization of the above and the below within the Tree."

"The Tree connects masculine and feminine," I said, "so by working with this Tree men and women can heal their relationships." Nodding "Yes," the Grandmothers said, "Invite women and men to come to do this work together. This work will balance yin and yang.

"We will teach this though you," they said. "The Tree of Life is the world Tree; it *is* the world. The roots of the Tree embrace every part of the earth and because of this, all beings are related. The Tree

nourishes and shelters everyone."

When I looked up I saw standing before me hundreds of people from the all the races and nations of the world. As I observed their customs and costumes I saw how this Tree belonged to each of them.

"Love everyone," the Grandmothers said. **"Visualize the roots of this Tree as veins of the great rivers of the world, reaching into every country on earth—Europe, Asia, Africa, the Americas, all islands and the poles. These roots touch everything. The roots of the Tree intertwine within the earth and its branches shelter all."**

Again they showed me the core group and I watched as each one approached the Tree. **"They are searching for their root/route,"** the Grandmothers said. **"Your root/route anchors you in a perfect way for the being that you are."**

As everyone walked forward the Grandmothers demonstrated how their lives followed a particular root/route. Like the Tree's roots, their life's route journeyed down to its Source too. After they reached their Source, they traveled back up into the body of the Tree where they bloomed, ripened, and then finally dropped from the Tree, their energy flowing back into earth. This, in short, was the cycle of human life.

The teachings of the Tree of Life were elegant, economical and so complex that I could grasp only a small portion of this archetype. When I struggled to comprehend more of it, I began to get dizzy. **"Rest,"** the Grandmothers said, **"you must learn at the right pace."**

I invited men and women to come to the garden to practice the Tree of Life exercises. We would first harmonize the energies of yin and yang inside ourselves, and then work to bring this balance to earth.

On the patio I set up an altar representing different forms of the Divine. My husband and son took part in this event, women from the core group arrived and other people I didn't know came too. When a man from the homeless group I fed every Thursday walked through the gate I smiled. This was a typical Grandmothers' gathering; I had had no knowledge of who would show up.

After explaining the Grandmothers and their purpose, I introduced the concept of the Tree of Life and we discussed the gap in understanding between men and women. Everyone present was sincere in her/his desire to seek a better relationship with herself/himself and the opposite sex.

After we practiced breathing from the roots, then the branches of the Tree, we felt the expansion of our great *Self*. Then we honored the balance and harmony of yin and yang within and around us.

The afternoon was a great success, and when it was over a burly man raised his hand and tearfully asked me, "Is there anything I can do to help the Grandmothers?" His question brought tears to my eyes too, and, not knowing what else to say, I asked him to simply call on them. The longing he expressed made me see just how deeply men, as well as women, have suffered from the imbalance between yin and yang.

CHAPTER 17

Make Your Lives Sacred

"Giving from the Heart leads to further reception. Other kinds of giving are not giving at all."

The next time I returned to the upper world I just wanted to be with the Grandmothers and the holy man. The depth of this work was drawing me ever closer to these great beings.

I took my seat on the dais with them and sat in silence, gazing out over the world where in the distance the Grandmothers pointed out **"the great ones."** They were referring to two manifestations of the Divine that were visible on the horizon. Narrowing my eyes, I recognized the form of the Virgin Mary and that of Lord Krishna, the Hindu god and avatar.

Each form was wafer-thin and looked like a piece of colored cellophane, overlaying an *enormous* light. Light shone through the form, shimmered around it and created such a glare that I had to concentrate to focus on the "cellophane." Mary's form was in pinks and blues while Krishna's was all blue. Each was a prism, a place for the light to shine through.

The light was overpowering. Blinding me, it covered the visual field, so thoroughly flooded it, that it was impossible to discern anything except light. Light—so total you didn't see it. Both foreground and background—light was everything, and a brilliant glare over all.

These forms provided a focal point, gave the light of the Divine color and form. Because a blinding over-all light blankets everything, it is difficult to see; a form is easier to look at. Once I understood this I spent the entire journey gazing in rapture at Mary and Krishna, so grateful to the Divine for providing these forms (of the formless) for us to relate to and love.

As I transcribed this journey I realized that the Grandmothers have put the radiant light into yet another form. This time the Divine has revealed Itself as wise old women, comforting and easily accessible to all.

"Let our teaching fall on the waters of their lives and make ripples suitable to them."

Two days after seeing the oneness of God in the light underlying the forms of Mary and Krishna, I received an anonymous letter saying that I wasn't fit to do the Grandmothers' work. Obviously sent by a woman who had taken part in an empowerment ceremony, it expressed anger with me for presuming to speak for the Grandmothers. She listed some of my flaws and although I was aware of the ones she mentioned, receiving a letter like this shocked me.

A few days later, two women in the core group started teasing me about being "special" for my relationship with the Grandmothers. Their responses and the critical letter took me by surprise and made me self-conscious. How, I wondered, would I deal with criticisms like these when the work went out to larger groups?

When I asked the Grandmothers how to deal with criticism and jealousy, they said, **"Our message needs to go out, but you do not.**

"Removed," they said. **"This is *our* message; you are the messenger. That is all."** Relief flooded me as I listened. I was only the messenger. **"You are not the target and must not be,"** they said. **"Our work cannot be personal. If it is, others will do as she who wrote the letter did—pick apart your flaws, and ascribe them to us. You are only parlaying our message. *It is not about you.*"** Looking serious they said, **"It must not be—for your sake and ours'.**

"As you write, keep the writing personal enough so it is clear that this message came through a person. Give the teachings, then move back and keep your own counsel. Let our teachings fall on the waters of their lives and make ripples suitable to them.

"Share what it is like as learning comes to you as it does. Your experience will anchor their experiences and give them confidence, but this is not your story."

I was not to share as much of myself as I had. No more detailing how a recent teaching had affected me, nor was I to share much personally in the book. It was distracting. This guideline would keep the focus on the Grandmothers.

Suddenly I was viewing this conversation from off in the distance. In this scene I was fading. I looked smoky, grayed out and indistinct, like the background of a painting. **"You are our messenger,"** the Grand-mothers said. **"Say that."** They were showing me that I was far from the centerpiece of this story.

"It is woman's nature to be beautiful and love beauty."

I decided to take a break from giving empowerments and from group meetings. Before I resumed I wanted to learn how to stay in the background and keep my own counsel. All my life I had been self-dis-closing, now I needed to build new habits.

What did the Grandmothers want me to do during this time of inner focus? I began my journey with this question in mind and on my way to them, Eagle appeared. **"Get on, Kid,"** he growled, a tough guy with a heart of gold. I climbed on his back and when we reached the Grandmothers as soon as I slid off, they laughed and pulled me toward them. Swinging my arms in sync with theirs, we swung along like child-hood playmates.

They wanted me to be one of them. A Grandmother. They had told me this the second time we met but somehow I had forgotten their invi-tation. How could I forget such a thing? I wondered. Was I afraid to be a Grandmother?

As they drew me into their circle I looked at them up close. They were so young! Not old, not wizened, these young women were the Grandmothers! Seeing their youthful smiles dazed me, made me feel woozy and light-headed. But nodding to confirm that what I was seeing was true, they drew me in even closer, and we danced together, young Grandmothers all.

As we wove in and out, round and round, I couldn't look at any-thing but them. How vibrant they were! Laughing at me, they pointed, suggesting I take a look at myself, so I glanced to the side and saw my reflection. I was young too! We all were, just a bunch of fun loving kids dancing in a circle.

"I need to get my hair back off my face," I said, "that's how they're wear-ing theirs." I was even thinking like a kid, wanting to look like them.

They combed my hair and made me beautiful, made me one of them. **"Power is beauty. Beauty is power,"** they chanted as they motioned to me, saying, **"rise up."** We had been standing together but now we lifted up, ascending until at last we stood in the air, far above the ground.

"The upper world is such a different dimension, not at all like earth," I said, as I watched it from this point, midair. There were trees just as there were on earth; there were mountains, rivers, and cities. Much of what I saw resembled the beauty we see on earth, but earth felt constricting by comparison. As I looked out over the varied beauty of this plane, it seemed to go on and on forever.

"**Stay with us,**" the Grandmothers said and I jolted awake from a sleep I hadn't realized I was entering. Awake again, now I saw movement and sparkling light in front of me. The Grandmothers were bringing out headdresses, each one standing about two feet tall. These were made of intricately worked gold and were covered in gems. As they fitted one on my head I hardly felt it. It was made of light. Ancient in appearance, these headdresses were light in every way. And when they placed one on my head the world became magical. Showered with jewels, I was covered with a dazzling light that made everything glow.

"**Women love beauty,**" they said. "**It is woman's nature to be beautiful and love beauty.**" They turned and pointed to a stork-like bird that was stalking through high grass with its wings folded. As I watched its graceful strides they said, "**You are seeing this bird's nature.**" It dawned on me that the bird was like me, tall, with long legs and a small head, and I turned to the Grandmothers and asked, "I'm supposed to observe my own nature, then follow it. Is this the message?" They beamed at me, proud that I figured this out on my own.

"How can I learn about my nature?" I asked and waited for them to speak, but there was only silence and so I returned to the purpose of my journey. "Grandmothers, what would you have me do during this time?" I asked.

"**Play with us,**" they said. My mouth flew open. What? Catching the expression on my face, they roared with laughter, delighted by surprising me. "**From this moment on, we want you to include us in** *everything* **you do,**" they said. "**No more thinking of us only when you have a question or need help.**"

They wanted to go shopping with me, walk the dog, and work with clients, cook, and plant the garden. I was to do it all with them. I felt honored.

They placed me inside a pale blue cylinder, and I felt safe and glad to be there. This place was protected. Filled with light, it filled me with light. As I saw and felt jewels from the headdresses raining down inside the cylinder I heard the Grandmothers say, "**Light heart.**" When again I asked what they wanted me to do during this time they said, "**Light hearted.**" This was how they wanted me to be.

Now they spread their wings and covered me, and the movement of their feathers created a warm breeze that lifted my hair in a caress.

"**Receive**," they whispered, as they fanned me. They explored my back and shoulders with the tips of their wings and lovingly touched the sore points there. Then they covered me with a feathered cape to which they were also attached. "**Come back to us, come to us**," they said.

"Make your lives sacred.

After this journey I started to *really* enjoy myself, just hanging out with the Grandmothers. Once I made the choice to be with at all times, information seemed to come to me from out of the blue. Life and its every-day tasks became easier.

Living with the Grandmothers each day was wonderful, but whenever I had a specific question for them, one that required more than a brief response, I still journeyed to the upper world. A formal question seemed to demand a journey. I had noticed that the Grandmothers imbued their teachings with ceremony and now I wanted to understand why. This was the focus of my next journey.

When I stepped before them to ask my question I sensed more joy than usual. They were happy, but it was more than this. My mood, my very body lifted as I came into their presence. "Grandmothers what would you like me to write about the importance of ceremony in daily life?" I asked. As they stood back and regarded me, I understood that they had waited a long time for this question.

They formed the familiar circle and as they closed ranks, they said, "**Ceremony is part of life; it is a mindful interacting with the sacred within life. It is not much present in your world today**," they added, "**and you suffer from this. Everyone suffers its loss—plants, people, everything.**" Shaking their heads they said, "**You don't know how to have fun and life is hard for you. Everything on earth would support you if you would but enter in with it.**

"**Look up the word, ceremony**," they said. "**Ceremony has to do with recognizing the sacredness of life at every moment.**" I looked up ceremony as soon as I returned from this journey, but the dictionary definition was about procedure, not about its original purpose. And although "religion" was mentioned in the definitions I found, the word sacred was not.

"**Ceremony brings pleasure into life**," the Grandmothers said. "**There is nothing arcane or difficult about it. It is joyful. Ceremony affirms the moment; it affirms the precariousness and the importance of each act.**"

Cocking their heads to the side, bemused, they said, **"You live today as though you were the first to *ever* do anything."** Their expressions showed how arrogant they found this attitude. **"You live in the illusion that you are the first to have had such and such a thought or to have moved in such a way, or to have made such a mental association."** Laughing at our ego-centered view, they appeared astonished by our isolation from the past, our lack of connection with those who have gone before us, and by our failure to use ceremony to acknowledge and celebrate these connections.

"You are not the first," they said. **"You are warp and woof of the great pattern of life. Your ancestors knew this. The bark of the tree knows this. Your DNA knows this! Why then do you make your lives so hard?"**

I stood, bewildered, and they looked at me with loving understanding. **"It is your ego,"** they said, **"you have chosen this isolated view of life because it makes you feel important."** Brushing their hands together as if dusting them clean, they said, **"When you are tired of feeling important and want to be happy, come back to ceremony. Enjoy the life in ceremony,"** they said, twelve heads nodding as one, **"and let the *life within ceremony* support you."**

Leaning forward, they warmed to their topic. **"Saying grace before meals is a ceremony of reverence. Blessing your food—a reverential act. Blessing seeds as you plant them, thanking your car, blessing your car, holding your steering wheel in reverence."** They glanced up as they said this and broke into laughter when they saw my expression. Collapsing into one another, holding their sides, some of them were laughing so hard they were crying.

It was my reaction to **"hold your steering wheel in reverence,"** that was convulsing them. **"Don't you see?"** they asked, wiping their eyes, **"There is nothing that is not sacred."** "Okay, Grandmothers, okay, even the steering wheel."

"Gathering with friends for a purpose that fosters good is a sacred act, greeting the dawn with prayer is ceremony. As simple acts like these are done repeatedly, their repetition creates ceremony.

These then take on life of their own; this is how ceremony supports you. Sitting in the same chair, on the same cushion, in the same spot to pray or meditate each day is ceremony." The cushion or chair would begin to carry a charge. Whenever we saw it, we would think, "Meditate," and when we sat down on it, the process of meditation would automatically begin.

"You are not alone," they said. **"You suffer *needlessly* from this delusion. We are always with you. Always. Come together in groups of**

sisterhood," they urged, "in groups of brotherhood, in family groups where like minds and open hearts gather and there do ceremony. Send blessings and prayers for others. Such acts are ceremony," they smiled as if to say, "Now isn't this easy?" "Chants, songs, prayers—these are offerings you can send forth. They create ribbons of light that go out over the earth, over all the world!

"You are missing the *joy of life,* you struggle alone if you have no ceremony. Many are SO TERRIFIED of believing in the Divine that they choose to live in self-imposed loneliness." Denying our connection to the sacred cuts us off from the Source. The looks on the Grandmothers' faces showed how they had grieved this self-imposed distress that some people place on themselves.

"A ceremony upon arising," they said, "a simple prayer or body posture that invokes the directions of the earth and the spirits of the land. Saying a prayer from any of the world's religions—all of these are *beautiful.*" Leaning forward, eyes wide as if to say "Pay attention," they said, "You wake each day because of grace. Recognize this. Each day will have gifts and teachings in it—e-a-c-h day. Celebrate these gifts. You never know what the day will bring you!" Rubbing their palms together, they said, "There is excitement in that.

"A ceremony upon rising, a ceremony upon retiring, giving thanks for the day and for what you have received. Calling on the One, calling in the spirits to protect you as you sleep. They *will* do this," they said. Any form of the Divine we revere will protect us if we ask for protection. "*They,* the embodiments of the Divine, like to be remembered just as you do," they said and added, "Your life can become rich and *so much more* can be given to you if you but ask."

As they regarded me, they looked a bit like old-fashioned school-teachers. "Even little children are taught to say thank you," they said. "Shouldn't you do the same?" "Grandmothers," I interrupted, wanting to be sure I understood, "You want us to include the Divine in all that we do? In *everything*?" They looked at me with expressions that said, "Well of course."

"Make a sacred place where you can go to be with God, and it will support you over time. Each time you go there in reverence, the place will get stronger in support of you. You know what to say about this." I did know. The altar in our bedroom had supported me for a long time, so had the spot where the eagle had landed and the one under the fern trees where the empowerments were being held. Whenever I was away from home all I had to do was think of one of these places to feel peaceful and grounded.

"Gather together and send prayers for others and for one another," they said. "The generosity of spirit that comes from receiving from the highest and then giving to others will give you untold gifts." Seeming to glow, they said, "These acts light vortexes of light all over the earth.

"*It does not matter* **what form your prayers take,**" they said. "**It is the selfless giving to others, to one another, to all beings that matters.**" Speaking passionately they urged, "**Please do not get caught in the religiosity and rigidity of certain ways of doing things. But if you find a way that feels** *good* **and** *right* **to you, do it that way. But at the same time recognize that another has a way that is just as right and as good for her.**"

Expanding to their full height these towering Grandmothers said, "**Honor** *all paths* **to God, all paths to God. All colors are lovely, there are so many sounds in music, all prayers are beautiful, and so happily received.**"

"**Intention underlies everything,**" they said, gesturing widely. "**If a certain necklace is used over time with the intention of reverence, it will take on the energy of reverence. It will support the wearer. But without that intention, without the loving, sacred feeling toward it, the necklace will be nothing.**"

"**Ceremonies are legion,**" they said. "**Ma-a-any, m-a-any! Every culture that reveres the sacred has ceremonies and these are good. All are good,**" they said. "**You may choose any of them that you desire or make up your own. It is your intention that is important.**" Turning serious gazes on me they said, "**Say this.**"

They seemed to be looking me over. "**We have given you a mantle, a stola,**" they said and as they spoke something came to rest on my shoulders. It felt a little like the caul, but it only covered my chest and shoulders. Later I looked the word up in the dictionary. A stola is an ecclesiastic vestment.

"**Let each listen within the heart to the manner of reverencing the sacred that appeals to her or him. And don't be afraid,**" they said. "**Follow the inner inclination, whatever it may be. It may be Zen, it may be tribal, it may be the high mass, or it may be prayer at the mosque.** *It does NOT matter!*" they said. There is only one God and many paths to God. **But when you have chosen a path, then go with that one. Climb the mountain! Don't dabble around the edges, testing one thing and another.**" We can revere all paths to God, but to deepen our inner life, we must commit to one sacred practice and stick with it.

"**Climb the mountain on the pathway that is right for you,**" they said, "**joining in ceremony with others of like mind along the way,** ceremonies of thanksgiving, ceremonies of repentance, of forgiveness, of joy, or of release. Ceremony is for you and it is also to share with others of like mind. Ceremony will nourish and strengthen you."

Their faces softened and they said, "We bless you. We bless each one who nourishes and strengthens the sacred within.

"Pray together," they said, "asking for wisdom and healing. Pray for one another and send prayers to those who are not physically present but who need them. As you step toward God, God steps toward you," they assured me, "but you must take that step. Ceremony helps you do that. A ceremony with a powerful intention travels straight to God." They paused, giving me a look of love so complete that tears came to my eyes. "A ceremony with a powerful intention, God is there in such ceremony.

"Greet the dawn in this way, and throughout the day think of us or of whatever form of the Divine you revere. Think of us as you work, as you travel to and from your work, as you eat your meal, as you prepare your meal. Always think of the Divine and call on the Divine. *Let your lives be filled with the presence of the Divine.*"

Boring their eyes into mine, they said, "Make your lives sacred. You must take this step. This is the time to do this. Do not wait. There is momentum building now, and great power. This momentum will return you to the sacred and your life will become joyous and full of peace. This we say to you."

As the drumbeat signaled my return I was suffused with emotion, tears and a feeling of fullness in my chest. I turned to them and they said, "Come back soon."

On my way down, I reflected on what a surprise these journeys always were. This one could have been a book in itself. When I asked my question I expected a list of ceremonies to perform but the Grandmothers gave me nothing of the kind.

"When you pray an inclusive prayer it brings together every aspect of creation and blesses all life."

A few days later I returned to ask about ceremonies to include in the book and to thank them for the beauty of what they had shared on the last journey.

I rushed forward—so glad to be with them again, and from the looks on their faces I knew that they were just as glad to see me. "You

come here any time," they said, as they gently brushed the hair away from my forehead.

"Grandmothers," I murmured, my heart spilling devotion, "I want to be with you all the time." After we shared a loving look I said, "If there are specific ceremonies that would be helpful to others, especially at this time, I would like to pass them on."

"Watch," they said, and then moved to the side. A curtain behind where they had been standing parted to reveal a stage set. **"The scene is always changing,"** they said as I watched and waited.

"A gathering of the suns," they said, **"of the worlds, of the religions and of the peoples. Pray in an inclusive way,"** they said.

"When you pray, pray for all beings, excluding none. No outsiders, no 'us,' no 'them," they said. **"To all my relations' is a good prayer. 'May everyone in all the worlds be happy' is a good prayer. '*Inclusivity*,"** they said. **Now is the time for the end of division. Pray the prayer of *all* colors,"** they said, **"all are strands of light from the great source of light."**

As they spoke I saw people of every race and culture holding colored ribbons. Light, from the Source of all light, poured down these ribbons. This reminded me of the maypole exercise in Krystal's *Cutting the Ties that Bind*.

"Honor the colors of all peoples," the Grandmothers said, **"the specific perfection within each culture, religion and way of life—honor the perfection therein. No judgment,"** they said. **"Begin now to let judgment go. This is the beginning of the end of judgment of one another. Include prayers and chants that do this,"** they said.

"For those who feel themselves drawn to the Great Mother, the Memorare is a good prayer," they said. Here are the haunting words to this prayer.

"*Remember, O most holy Mother,*
That never was it known that one who fled to thy protection,
Implored thy help, or sought thy intercession was left unaided.
Inspired by this confidence, we fly to thee.
To thee we come, before thee we stand."

When I asked them for more ceremonies, they covered me with the cloak of feathers. This time it had a hood.

"Pray for the animals, pray for the plants, the rocks, the water and the air," they said. **"The Yoga salutation to the sun is a good prayer. Earth and heaven are brought together in this."**

"This is what you mean by inclusivity, isn't it, Grandmothers?" I said. "Such prayers harmonize yin and yang." **"Yes,"** they said, **"when** you pray an inclusive prayer it brings together every aspect of creation and blesses all life." Turning smiling faces to me they said, "That is why we have come—for the great harmonizing that heals.

"The purpose of all the prayers we have mentioned is to open your heart. As the heart opens, it becomes a bigger dwelling so that more of the Divine can come to live within you." Rolling their hands and wrists in circles, like small birds spiraling upward, they said, "And so it goes—on and on."

They gazed at me with melting tenderness and said, "This is why you were born." When I heard this, tears poured down my face. They had confirmed what I had always believed—that merging with God was the purpose of life.

"When you ask for blessings for yourself, include also the purpose of these blessings," they said, "that the blessing of self may radiate out to all beings. *Never pray only for your own tiny benefit,*" they said, "but recognize that whatever truly benefits you, will benefit all. This should always and will always be so. Other sorts of prayers are not prayers at all.

"Prayers and ceremonies of purification exist to cleanse the heart. The Divine enters *deeply* into the life of the one who prays like this and infuses her life with the sacred. She is blessed and these blessings move out from her to the entire world. Love in action comes from such prayers."

A searing pain shot into my temple and distracted me. For days I had lived with a sick headache and I was now becoming nauseated. "Grandmothers," I cried, "please!" Turning, they took me in their arms. "Much is changing within you, they said. "Much is shifting and realigning, a new balance and power. We will help you.

"There are no particular ceremonies," they said, responding to the question I had come with, "but the particular lesson for this time is inclusiveness. Therefore perform ceremonies that include and generously bless all beings, and ceremonies that ask for blessings for particular ones in order that they may serve all."

Spreading their arms so wide they looked like pelicans fanning their wings, they announced, "The GREAT EMBRACE. It is time for yin and yang to embrace." And as they turned to face me they said, "No more judgment but a reaching out, and an embrace of all."

I felt this embrace, this swelling of love inside and around me. I was part of everything that existed—I was soft, rounded, and enormous. I noticed that my headache was gone. "Pure intentions, pure ceremonies and prayers *do* create change within the body and within the psyche," they said. **"They create a greatness of being, an understanding and love of *all* creation."** This was what I was feeling.

Knowingly they smiled. **"When you feel this, let it flow out from you. This energy is food, manna; it feeds the hungry souls and hearts of the world. It will go to wherever it is needed,"** they said. **"You needn't think of a recipient—it will go wherever it is needed.**

"The meditations we have given, the Net of Light, the Fabric of Being, the Tree of Life and others, can be made into ceremony and done in groups or done alone," they said. These are inclusive and generous. *You cannot help yourself without helping others,"* they emphasized. **"You cannot be strengthened without strengthening the fabric of the world."**

On the way back to ordinary reality I reviewed this journey. "There are no specific ceremonies for this time in history, but there is a specific lesson and that is inclusiveness," I said. "Also generosity. As you give and are given to, everything benefits."

CHAPTER 18

It Is Time

"Go slow, go deep. You will find us there within you, around, behind, and under you."

On my next journey, no sooner had I arrived before the Grandmothers than one of them took my hand and walked me to a cliff where we peered over what seemed to be the edge of the world. On the horizon I made out our own blue planet, just as the astronauts' famous photograph shows it. But even at this distance, I could see that something strange was taking place on earth. Superimposed on the planet were figures turning on a wheel.

The figures grappled with one another as the wheel arced, its evolution rolling them upside down and sideways, contorting them into odd shapes and strange movements, but still they hung on. This was the human struggle, our attempt to grasp at and control fate that makes the wheel of life turn. It looked like a wrestling match to me. As the figures fiercely battled for control, it was their struggle that turned the wheel.

"**Keep watching,**" the Grandmothers said, and as they spoke I became aware of the sun's disk-like shape underneath and behind all this movement of the wheel.

"**Sink into yourself, sink into your divine nature,**" they said. "**If the sun were not providing light, you wouldn't be able to see movement at all, would you?**" they asked. "**But *all* you see is movement.**"

With difficulty I pulled my gaze away from this drama of earth, sun and wheel and focused on the Grandmothers. "**You do not recognize the light, the presence of God that overlies, underlies, surrounds and fills all of life,**" they said. "**All you see is movement! SHIFT YOUR FOCUS to the light!**"

It wasn't easy to look only at the sun. That wrestling match on the wheel kept distracting me. Without the sun's light I wouldn't have been able to see anything, but the sun wasn't *doing* anything! It was hard to focus on it because my eyes were drawn to *action*.

"We give stories and the journeys that produce these stories to create a shift in your perspective," the Grandmothers said, **"to break your old focus on action. Here, on the physical plane, the focus on action creates a limitation."**

As they spoke I saw shadow puppets and noticed that as they moved they created a flat sort of reality of dark against light. There was no depth to the "reality" they produced; it was just a small flat movement. **"*This* is what you see,"** the Grandmothers said.

"Life is not a series of flat, linear movements, movements for example into buying a house, taking a job, having a child. That is not, THAT is not life," they said. **"Those are *activities* on the surface of life."** They searched my face to see if I understood. **"Sink deep within yourself,"** they said, **"sink *down* into yourself."**

I turned my attention inward and felt myself slowing, especially my mind. It had been racing. **"Feel yourself, and know that all activity of body and brain is surface activity only. Surface, static, busyness and noise. It is neither important nor unimportant. Just activity.**

"Feel your body *now*!" they commanded and I focused on my breath, on the sensation of warmth inside me. **"No more foolish living,"** they said. **"No more rushing from stimulation to stimulation. *That*,"** they said, **"is foolish living. Actually that is not living at all.**

"The purpose of life is to recognize who you are, to recognize the presence of the Divine everywhere and move below the surface of things, into the flow of knowing what all is." I listened intently. **"When you do this we can come to you,"** they said. **"When you do this we are *with* you."**

All was quiet for a minute or two and then I began to hum low in my throat. Hummmmmm. **"This,"** they said, **"is the vibration of your being. Be in that vibration. This is how to receive our teaching. Moving into the vibration of your being creates a shift within you, creates a new perception of and reception to life. You will be different. You will be wise."** Smiling, they said, **"Wise is very different from smart. Oh, you may still be smart,"** they said with a laugh, **"but you will be wise."**

I wanted to understand this distinction between wise and smart. It seemed like one of them involved effort while the other did not. **"Do not be confused,"** they said. **"The desire for action will not bring you happiness. What we are speaking of is a *different* sort of doing. It is not rushed and busy; it is not a piling up of accomplishments. It is not a list of projects or a busy social calendar. It is none of these.**

"Those activities," they said, giving me a look of infinite patience, "are yang. The emphasis on yang values has created the tension, stress and difficulty on your planet. We have not come for that," they said, shaking their heads. "We have come to help balance that."

Turning the intensity of their gaze on me, they said, "We ask you to go deep, to do what you do with love in your heart. We ask you to look outward from your heart at the people in your lives. To do this," they said, "you must first go deep inside yourself and feel your body, feel that low hum inside you. This is the vibration of life. The same vibration that flows through the trees, through the people sitting next to you, through the food you eat and the chair you sit on."

They gazed hard at me. "Relate from *this* place deep within your heart," they said. "And be brave!" they shouted, shooting fisted hands up to punch the air. "Don't be afraid. We are with you."

Laughing good-naturedly as they observed my stunned expression they said, "You can be yourself. You can! And you will nourish everyone. You will do so much good by being yourself, more than you ever did or could do by being busy and doing, doing, doing."

Looking me over, they said, "You are so cut off from what we are talking about that it seems to you we speak a foreign language. We can feel your apprehension and distrust of what we are saying." They regarded me so intently that love surged over me, and then said, "Oh, we bless you, and we do not lie. We will not desert you. It is true that you can live another way. You will bloom from within yourself; as you fill with love you will expand more than you ever dreamed you could."

I felt so happy and hopeful as I listened to them. "I want to live this way, Grandmothers," I said. "Go slow," they replied, "go deep. You will find us there within you, around, behind, and under you. The same as the light, the same as the air, as the warmth of the sun or the cool of the shade.

"This is a natural way of living," they said, "but you have lived in such an unnatural way for so long that when we speak this truth it sounds strange to you, you distrust it or think, 'That's not possible for me. How can I live like that? How can *anyone* live like that?'" They paused, "We tell you, you can. *It is time.* They were silent and then said, "As you begin to live like this, a shift is created for all beings.

"There is great power building now," they said. "The earth is your friend, your ally." They were serious, impassioned. "As you come awake to who you are, put your feet on the ground, put your hands in the grass, in the sand, in the dirt, or on the trees. Recognize the divine presence. The earth will help you open to who you are. The earth will help you to go deep; it will help you to go slow.

"When your mind wants to rush away with worry, with projects, lists, or anxiety, touch something of earth. Touch a plant, an animal, or touch your own body. Hold a piece of wood in your hands and remember from whence it came. The earth loves you and longs for your return to her. She longs for kinship with her children and some of you long for her too. Isn't it time?

"Go deep," they repeated, "go slow. And what you do will be beautiful. What you give you will truly give and from such giving you will receive wisdom and love, understanding and kinship with life. Your rewards will be enormous."

Cocking their heads, they said, "You needn't change your life, but to some degree you probably will. You will change your perspective," they said, "and remember that we are with you—always."

The drumbeat stopped, and then sped up. They hadn't directly answered my question, but they had given me new ways to look at the world and myself. With difficulty I said goodbye and as I returned to ordinary reality I noticed my chest, so full I could burst. I was shaken. Full of goodness and beauty and shaken by them too.

"Wisdom exists when the ego has been cleared away. Knowledge is particles stored by the ego."

For some time I had felt this work winding down. It was nothing the Grandmothers had said; it was more a feeling I had. I sensed a door closing. As soon as I realized this I put together a list of things I still wanted to understand. As I handed the Grandmothers my list I said, "I want to clarify any loose points, Grandmothers, and a question that keeps coming up has to do with the difference between wisdom and knowledge." They stood patiently, not really looking at me but brushing vague "stuff" off my shoulders and head.

"Don't worry," they said, and as they removed more from my back I noticed that it looked heavy, like a pile of debris. Finally they stopped working, lifted their hands above their heads and showed me the book, and holding it high, they polished it.

As I watched I heard them say, "The ego is hard to subdue," and instantly my chest grew hot. Heat shot to my cheeks as the thought flashed, "This is *my* work." I was horrified by my response, but the Grandmothers only smiled and repeated, "The ego is hard to subdue."

With their backs to me they huddled around my list while from out of nowhere, an enormous eagle, far larger than the one who had landed in our garden, swooped in. As he roared over my head, I caught the dark shape of his wings, then a flash of gold and heard, **"Thunderbird."**

Powerful wings pummeled me and swept debris from my mind and body. "Thank you!" I cried as the great bird swept away the fog in my mind—my questions too! I couldn't remember any of them. **"This is the dance of the thunderbird,"** the Grandmothers said as I watched him climb higher until I couldn't see his dark wings any more.

"Too full of self," they said. "Amen to that," I agreed, and again, flashing, crackling with power, broad wings swept my head and shoulders, dissolving my hold on the book and carried it away.

"This book is given," the Grandmothers said; **"you are only the channel. The book is given."** "Thank you," I shouted back, filled with the energy of the thunderbird. Power now coursed through the hidden places in my mind, washing away the blockages and clogged things in me.

"Wisdom exists when the ego has been cleared away," they said. "O-h," I whispered and started laughing. Here then was my lesson on the difference between wisdom and knowledge—made to order. They were removing my ego.

"Knowledge," they said, **"is particles stored by the ego—a stacking up of points for the benefit of the individual ego and for the ego of the race."** My struggle to 'figure out' the book was just this—an attempt to stack up points, each in its proper pile. **"Wisdom doesn't even remember itself,"** they said; **"it doesn't store anything. In wisdom is perfect freedom, and in freedom is wisdom.**

"Striving to acquire wisdom will never achieve it," they said. **"Love alone brings wisdom while wisdom begets a deeper love."** Leaning in close, they confided, **"Wisdom is not of the mind; it is of the heart."** To illustrate, they said, **"You can sense a wise person but such a one is hard to describe because it is your mind that does the describing. The mind by its nature parcels out and compartmentalizes."** "Of course," I thought. "How can something as limited as the mind describe something as unlimited as wisdom?"

Smiling, they said, **"Love more. Seek to be shown *how* to love. Seek to love everyone, to love all of life more and more. Seek that, and when you feel that love, let yourself bask in it.**

"Such love brings wisdom and along with wisdom comes infinite intelligence. This is the deep, knowing intelligence of the heart which is cosmic in its power, cosmic in its reach." Nodding and rocking on their heels, they said, "This is a very desirable state to live in. Those who achieve wisdom are happy.

"Take the opportunity to love," they said. "Choose to love and embrace the good in each. Embrace the *actual* being in each one." Raising a finger to get my attention they said, "Do not be distracted by behavior." I was to look beyond the obvious, to the person underneath the behavior. "You are given opportunities each day to see the good and to allow love to open you. Take those opportunities! This is how you will grow in love, wisdom, and freedom.

"It is the ego that wants to compartmentalize, because this gives the ego the illusion of control. The ego is limited in its understanding, but with a little knowledge it can fool itself into believing that it is more than it is.

"Seek wisdom," they said. "You will be given the right amount of knowledge in order to apply this wisdom, but seek wisdom above all. And you will find wisdom through the avenue of loving.

"Acquiring wisdom," they said, "has to do with harmonizing yin and yang. A state of deep wisdom is a state of deep love. In such a state there are no polarities. The embrace of wisdom is too great for dualism. Wisdom goes beyond division; it is all-inclusive in its embrace.

"Look for the thing you can love in each one. Good is magnified through this act and wisdom then settles in and expands over all."

I bowed before them and unperturbed; they reached over my head to remove more debris from my back—handfuls of it. What they were removing was part of my ego, a part that had been trying to hold on to things, to categorize and control. And oh, the pain this holding on had created. Each block or pile on my back was heavy and stabbed me somewhere along my spine. Although I had never known it, this debris had been a heavy load to carry.

When I turned my awareness inside myself I saw two separate states there. Knowledge was the first. Upright, it was formed of stacks—knowledge upon knowledge upon knowledge—like a building assembled from multiple storage units. Inside me stood a great stack of knowledge, tall and listing a little to one side.

I saw wisdom too but wisdom didn't rise up as high. It was also rectangular, but more horizontal than vertical, and somewhat rounded at the edges. More of wisdom touched the ground than stood in the air. It had a color too—blue, where knowledge looked gray or perhaps colorless.

As I watched, the structure or rectangle of wisdom embraced that of knowledge, wrapped itself around it and seemed to include it with itself. Wisdom was active.

If we were to call wisdom a building, then the building of wisdom had wings that extended on each side, and these encircled the building of knowledge. It was these wings that created the movement I saw. Wisdom was comfortable with itself, also comfortable with knowledge. Since wisdom was inclusive, not exclusive, wisdom and knowledge went well together. But knowledge alone was a precarious edifice; stacked up so tall it wasn't stable. But when wisdom encircled knowledge and supported it, knowledge grew steady.

I looked at the Grandmothers. "So it's not wrong for a person to seek knowledge as long as it is sought from a perspective of wisdom," I said. Since they said nothing, I went on. "The quest for knowledge needs to come from the desire to love, to serve and understand. If we love and understand, knowledge will 'stand." **"Yes,"** they said.

Smiling at one another we formed a circle and swayed back and forth, like trees blowing in a breeze. Gracefully our heads tipped left, our heads tipped right. Then the Grandmothers swirled around me, and dancing in and out, wrapped me in something silky and blue.

As I left their realm and returned to ordinary reality, I was still wrapped in this blue mantle, blue, the color of wisdom.

"We come, we come when you call us."

The Grandmothers had answered my questions, at least those I could think of. But still wondering if there was anything in their message I had not yet recorded, I journeyed to them once more.

I flew into their valley alone, dropped to the ground and prostrated before them. "I don't know why I did that," I said, but I was face down on the ground and my body would not get up.

Laughing, they lifted me high in the air, and rising off the ground with me, in the air we performed a little minuet together. As we danced midair, out of the corner of my eye I noticed the wire of my microphone dangling before me. "What is my microphone doing here?" I asked. "Are we in ordinary or non-ordinary reality?" **"Who cares?"** came the answer.

"Grandmothers, is there anything, you want women to do with your message that you haven't yet told me?" I asked. They seemed to think this over, then turned to me and said, **"Come."**

They wore skirts that seemed to float around their bodies and as they walked ahead of me they reminded me of long-legged birds with multi-colored plumage. They broke into dance and began to circle and weave with one another.

Creating shifting patterns and colorful forms they swayed together as the clouds above them glided over the earth. I didn't know if the Grandmothers were following the clouds, or if the clouds were following them, but the designs of sun and shade that rippled over their brilliant skirts were magnificent. Movement, patterns of light and dark, everywhere I looked was fluidity and harmony. The Grandmothers were performing the dance of life.

As they dipped and swirled I glimpsed the contrast between their graceful movements and the background of compacted earth on which they danced. The ground underneath their feet was sectioned into parcels; solidified and packed so tightly it looked like bricks.

They taught me how to dip and sway with them, and my skirt, along with theirs, began a waltz-like rhythm. Gently it tapped the ground and knocked against the deadened condition of the earth. Each time one of our skirts swept the ground it jostled the compaction of the earth. The rhythm of our skirts tapping the ground was so enticing, so natural; it made the stuck material of earth *want* to move with it.

As I heard the old "Blue Skirt Waltz," I thought "How lovely it is to swing and flow like this." Oh, the beauty of this dance that was calling everything into harmony.

The earth beneath my feet began to vibrate. No longer rock solid, it now thrummed. I felt a breeze and as I looked up I saw shrubs blowing and bowing to one another. Not only I, but the entire natural world, was following the Grandmothers' lead in this dance of life.

"How are we who hear your message to use it?" I asked them. **"Allow yourselves to move in grace,"** they answered. **"Allow yourselves to dance and trust the grace within you. Trust the grace within your life."**

"Grandmothers, my dear ones, how are we to use your message?" I repeated, wanting more now that this phase of my work with them was ending. **"In joy!"** they called out, **"Use our message in joy, and *trust* in the rhythm of life.**

"This is not a hostile world," they said. **"Excessive yang energy has made it seem so, but this is not its nature. Harmony underlies the yang excesses on earth. Trust in this underlying harmony and do not fear. Do not,"** they said, wagging a finger, **"go into gloom and doom and Armageddon. No!"** they cried, stamping their feet. They were fierce, these bird-like Grandmothers in multi-colored plumage.

"Trust in the rhythm of life," they said, **"and *dance* with life! Put yourself into harmony with it. *Listen*," they said, "and life will lead you in the dance. Let life lead," they said and, catching the look on my face as I considered what it might be like if I were to "let life lead," they laughed.

"Listen to what life is telling you," they said. "See what life brings you every day and notice how that feels.

"What do you resonate with?" they asked, and pausing, said, "Go with that. That is the rhythm of life." I was beginning to see what they meant. "It *is* a friendly world," they said. "Earth below and sky above, trust in these. You are in your right place.

"Remember how much you are *loved!*" they said, "and as you remember this, you will love more." Flinging their arms wide they declared, "More love will pour through you—constantly! You will be happier and happier as you dance with life and life dances with you."

They began to sing and their song made me cry. Two lines, "Oh, how we love you. Oh how we love you," sung over and over. "Sing this to the women and men," they said, "and have them sing it too. The next time the group comes together, sing this song. It will put them into greater harmony with us and with one another.

"You have done a good job. We bless you," they said and my heart was so full I could not speak. "*Let* your hearts be full," they said, responding to my state, "for it is true that we love you deeply, fully and always. Let us fill you."

I felt filled full, fulfilled, I felt it all. I watched as they blessed the book and holding it on its bottom edge, knocked it three times against the hardened ground. Pom, pom, pom!

Then they looked at me and said, "It is time for you to fly down." "I will, Grandmothers," I promised, gazing at them, but I didn't want to go. I never wanted to leave them again, but as this thought came I saw their stern looks.

I turned back to them once more before I lifted off. They sent their love to me in their smiles and said, "We come; we come when you call us. Whether you call us alone or whether you call us in a group, we come. Know this. Let your lives be imbued with the presence of the Divine. It is yours for the asking.

"This is a proper ending for this book," they said and blowing me a kiss, added, "We are waiting for you. Turn to us. Call on us. We wait for your call."

CHAPTER 19

The Grandmothers' Workbook

"These meditations anchor our teachings, allowing them to go deep into the viscera of your body/mind."

Mental understanding provides only a limited grasp of the truth. To give a visceral understanding of the truths they have come to impart, I have gathered the Grandmothers' meditations and visualizations here.

Their teachings have layers of meaning. That is why the Net of Light, Fabric of Being, Tree of Life and others are given in symbolic form. Symbols do not confine, but rather, expand the mind. **"These,"** the Grandmothers explain, **"are tools for furthering individual empowerment."** Whether or not you have chosen to receive the Grandmothers' empowerment, these tools will help you put their work into practice. **"These meditations anchor our teachings, allowing our lessons to go deep into the viscera of your body/mind and be held there. Then they can become your own truth.**

"When you have owned and taken in these truths, they will no longer be thoughts that pass through your mind but will be deeply known." These meditations create change. Not intellectual exercises, they are opportunities to experience another way of being.

They transform the one using them and from her, go on to create change for many. Telling us, **"Never underestimate the power of these exercises,"** the Grandmothers say, **"Great good comes from your seemingly simple efforts."**

This part of the book is a workbook for those wanting an active part in this work. The meditations are scattered throughout the book but I have brought them together here for easier access and fuller explanation. Some are simple, some complex, but each will help you heal and balance yourself. And, just as important, they will bring healing and balance to the earth.

There is a saying that goes "I hear and I forget, I see and I forget, but

I experience and I remember." Meditations and visualizations follow the path of experience, enabling us to by-pass the critical mind so we can learn something new. You may wish to read these aloud or tape-record them so you can listen directly to the power in the Grandmothers' words.

PRELIMINARY RELAXATION EXERCISE

If you are unfamiliar with meditating, this simple method will bring you to a point of relaxation and provide an entry for work with the Grandmothers. Use it as needed to precede the specific meditations.

To begin, find a place where you can be alone, take a seat and once you have, think of why you have taken this seat. What is it you want from this experience? You may be curious about these so-called Grandmothers or you may want to open yourself to the presence of the Divine. Be clear about what you seek as you approach this work. Your clarity honors them and you. *This is your intention.*

Once you have taken your seat, let your body assume an open position. Uncross your hands and feet, unless you are sitting cross-legged on the floor. Take a moment to notice how perfectly the chair or floor supports you. They support us at every moment though we are seldom aware of it. Feel your contact with the chair or floor and notice how comfortable or uncomfortable you are.

How is your body occupying space? Where is its weight placed? Notice all parts of your body. Are your feet heavy on the floor? Do you feel your feet? Take the time you need to settle in and observe what is taking place inside you with a somewhat disinterested air, like taking inventory. Is your heart beating fast or slow? Is the rhythm of your breath regular or irregular? *Just notice.*

Take a slow, deep breath and as you exhale, think of letting go of the old (old thoughts, old attitudes, old air) and when you inhale think of absorbing the new. Close your eyes and do this three or four times. Feel your breath moving in and out with a deep, slow rhythm. *Letting go of the old, opening to the new.*

Observe the way your heart is beating and notice its rhythm. Is it slowing down? Speeding up? What is the temperature of your body? Your heart may beat fast or steadily. Your body may feel warm or cool. You may be tense or relaxed as you begin, but don't try to change anything about yourself. Don't force yourself to "try" to relax. Simply observe without judging yourself. *Observe and take your time.*

Notice where your body is tight and where it feels softer, if you are holding your breath or breathing fast or slow. No judgment. No hurry. *Just keep observing* without evaluating yourself. When at last you begin to relax, you can let the Grandmothers know you are ready to work with them.

MEDITATION ON THE NET OF LIGHT

"The light that illumines the net originates in the heart of each one."

To experience the Net of Light, think of, imagine or sense a sparkling Net of Light, like a great fishing net that covers the entire world. As you think of this Net notice that you are attached to it, a point of light on the Net. Feel, sense, see or imagine your connection.

As you make your connection, you will become aware of strands of light moving from person to person all over the earth. It is this connection that creates this Net or web. Hold this thought and observe your response to it. How are you attached to the Net? Where are you placed? Don't question your observations—*just observe*. Questioning at this point ties the mind in knots and stops the flow of meditation.

Drawing a picture of the Net can make its image clearer. Some visualize when they do an exercise like this, some conceptualize and others sense things. As you begin, notice how you experience the Net of Light. If you are not a visual type you can simply think of it and imagine your connection to it. Since your energy always follows wherever you send thought, thinking of the Net is enough to bring it into being.

To activate your place in the Net of Light, inhale its light for four or five breaths. Feel or think of your place in the Net while you breathe and notice how your body responds. **"As consciousness of your place in the Net awakens and becomes stable, you may feel the effervescence from this lighted Net moving through the veins of your body."** You may experience a movement of light inside you now because the Net is inside as well as outside you. You are part of it just as it is part of you.

Responses to the Net are beautiful. Some see or sense light illuminating their body. Some feel joy or peace, while most feel loved and comforted by this connection. No matter what you experience, by thinking of the Net, once you activate your place in it, you are part of it.

"The light that illuminates the Net originates in the heart of each one." The Net is not external because **"the Net is lit by the jewel that each one is."** Everyone who participates in this meditation gives love and support to the Net, becomes part of the on-going flow of giving and receiving light. Light, broadcast along the lines of the Net, quickly returns to the sender through her senses. **"Your hearts make the decision to generate light. This is then pumped into the world through the strands of the Net. After that, it is your eyes, ears and breath that bring to you the gift of returning light."**

Think of sending light from your heart through the strands of the Net and notice how love and light follow your thought, moving into the world. You are more powerful than you have ever imagined. It is your own heart that generates the light of this Net and your thought of connection with the Net of Light that transmits it.

Sending light through the network takes place effortlessly; no sooner do you think of it than light moves forth. Experience the transmission of light along the increasingly lighted network that you are awakening, supporting, and which is in turn supporting you.

You are part of the Net of Light, a living system that supports the earth. It is your own heart that generates the light of this Net and your heart, pumping light with each beat that sends it forth. **"If you choose to give through your hearts, you will receive through your senses, and by this meditation on the Net of Light, goodness of every kind will be multiplied throughout the world."**

When I asked why light returns to the sender through her senses, the Grandmothers said, **"Light returns through your senses because humans receive in this way; this is how you know something is real. If information came only as a thought, you wouldn't believe it, would you? When something comes through your senses you record it physically, emotionally and mentally."**

CASTING THE NET OF LIGHT

To make the Net available to others, begin by calling on the Divine in any form, including that of the Grandmothers. Then think of the Net of Light and see or imagine yourself as part of it. Take a moment to experience the strength of the Net, feeling your connection to it before you continue. Then ask that it be cast to those who need it most and think of groups who especially yearn for this feeling of connection and support. The Grandmothers suggest that we send the Net to women first as, for the most part they will be the ones to hold the Net of Light for others.

Silently or aloud, name these groups, one at a time, and pause to experience the light from the Net going to each. When the core group works we usually cast the Net of Light in this order: to people in institutions (in hospitals, jails, etc.), to the elderly, to those living in poverty of any kind, to young people who are looking for a mentor and can't find one, to "successful," yang-based people, to all souls, especially the female souls, who are incarnating now to help with this work, and to all beings.

We cast to the elderly because they often feel passed over by the world. We cast to "successful," yang-based people (especially the women who need the support of their sisters) because these people are very much like the crazed bull—being run ragged by yang energy. We cast to all those who are suffering, whether physically, mentally or spiritually. Then we cast to all forms of life everywhere. We ask a blessing for all, ending this prayer/meditation with an ancient prayer. "May everyone in all the worlds be happy," we sing, repeating this three times.

This exercise can be changed as needed. You can vary to whom the Net of Light is cast or in what order, as everyone needs it and will benefit from connection to it. However, for the most part women are the ones who hold the Net steady, so to support the planet, when the core group meets, we cast to them first.

MEDITATION ON THE PITCHER AND THE CUP

"We do the Giving. You do the living."

To experience what it is like to have the Grandmothers fill you full of the Source, begin the same way you did in the previous exercises. Go to your quiet place and make yourself comfortable. Then call on the Grandmothers and ask them to take you to a sunny room where you can become acquainted with the Pitcher and the Cup. As soon as you make your request, a particular room will come to mind. Once it does, think of or see the table where the pitcher and cup sit. Sunlight streams over everything, pouring through a window, a doorway or another opening. See, sense, or imagine this.

Notice the pitcher—its size, shape, weight and color—and how full it is, full to the brim. Touch it if you like and feel its curves.

The cup, many times smaller, sits next to the pitcher. Take in the details of this scene as if you were an artist, capturing the size and shape of the table, the quality of light, color and shape of the cup and where it sits in relation to the pitcher. You may feel the warm sunlight, smell the air or hear the sounds of birds outside the window. Use your senses or imagination to create this scene and let it implant itself in your consciousness. Mark how you feel in this scene of light, grace and plenty.

Watch or think of the contents of the pitcher pouring into the cup, filling it full. When the Grandmothers gave me this exercise, the pitcher was full of cream but it can be full of any good thing. The Grandmothers may do the pouring or it may seem to take place by itself but as soon as the cup is full and the pitcher at rest, look inside. This pitcher *cannot be emptied*. It is kept ever filled by the Source.

Let yourself resonate to this. There is an endless supply here and you, at one with the sun-bathed pitcher, are filled to the brim too. A container of abundance and every good thing, that is what you are. You *cannot* be emptied because the Grandmothers will keep you ever filled.

"All you have to do to be filled is think of us," the Grandmothers say. **"As a result, you will find yourselves filled and, like the pitcher, there will be no room in you for emptiness. From this fullness, giving to others will take place so easily you won't even think of it as giving. There will be no separation between giver and given to. What you give will flow from the source of which you are a part."**

From a position of fullness, life flows effortlessly. The Grandmothers say, **"As you practice this exercise your life will become easier and easier—as it should be. We do the giving. You do the living, and let us give to others—through you."**

MEDITATIONS ON THE TREE OF LIFE

"You are related through this Tree."

To strengthen the relationship between women and men, and balance yin and yang the Grandmothers give us the Tree of Life meditations. **"The Mother cares not only for the branches or roots of the Tree but takes care of the whole Tree."** These meditations help us receive what we need from the feminine aspect of creation. With the re-emergence of yin comes an automatic increase in steadiness.

These meditations balance relationships and create harmony within individuals. They promote healing for the one meditating and for all life. **"The Tree of Life exercise is for everyone—men and women. Let yourselves experience the peace of this Tree."**

This meditation has three parts, each one valuable. But probably its greatest service lies in balancing the flow of yin and yang within oneself.

This is the world Tree, an archetype or symbol for unity and inter-connection, a subject of folk art around the globe, revered by indigenous peoples everywhere. I saw my first Tree of Life in Mexico—made of clay, with animals and people perched on its branches—but I have seen it since in many cultures.

"The symbol of the Tree serves a purpose. Its roots support every-thing in the world while its branches cover the earth. All beings are related to one another through this Tree. That is why 'Love everyone' is practical advice."

We are deeply joined with and by the energy of the Tree, which personifies our connection to God and one another. Although we live in a material world, we are more than base material. **"As you open to the support of God the Mother through the Tree of Life, you will have more to give. And as you learn to give in this way, you too will become a living and giving part of the Tree of Life."**

BALANCING YIN AND YANG

"You must realize that the Tree is a unit. Both above and below, roots and branches are one."

Since most people have a limited view of life, the Grandmothers teach us how to see the Tree not just as the sum of its parts, but as a whole. And to correct our perspective and awaken us to a balance of yin and yang, they give us a breathing meditation that harmonizes mas-culine and feminine energy. They use the symbol of the Tree to by-pass the limitations of our rational minds.

After you have relaxed, call on the Tree and observe as it comes to mind, being especially conscious of its canopy and roots. If you're not good at visualizing, *just call on the Tree.*

Think of, imagine, or feel yourself leaning against its trunk as you breathe deeply from its roots. Be aware of the entire Tree and notice your connection to it. You can do this sitting, standing, or lying down.

"Draw the energy of the earth up into your body with each breath, and do this three times." Receive whatever you need from Mother Earth with these three deep breaths—security, steadiness, and comfort—and observe as these gifts, specific qualities of the Great Mother, infuse your body and mind. Give yourself time to absorb them.

"Now breathe from the leaves and branches of the tree, drawing

the energy of the sky down into yourself with each breath. Do this three times." Draw in whatever you need from the masculine principle of energy—strength, protection and clarity.

Although we inhale first from the roots, and then from the branches, it is not necessary to direct our exhalations to anywhere in particular. "Your exhalation will go to wherever it is needed. Your in-breath carries with it a gift to you and your out-breath carries a gift to the world. These gifts will go where they are needed.

"Since breathing like this creates harmony within the self and forms a harmonious atmosphere, it will be beneficial for women and men to do this exercise together. It is absurd for men to ignore the feminine aspect of life or for women to ignore the masculine. If all of the branches of the Tree were cut, the Tree would die. If all of the roots were, cut the Tree would also die."

"The Tree needs attention and it needs care *now*." We can't afford to waste more time in power struggles; we must begin to view one another with new eyes. "The whole Tree needs care—both roots and branches. Great benefit will come from working with the Tree of Life. When you breathe like this, Earth and Sky meet in the great embrace of the Mother/Father, Father/Mother, yin/yang."

EXPANDING THOUGH THE ROOTS OF THE TREE

"This is the root/route for your life…
the Source for your individual life."

Following the relaxation procedure, visualize, imagine or think of the Tree's network of roots and branches, spreading farther than the eye can see. They encompass the earth, all peoples, their countries, and their customs. *Simply think this thought, let it go and observe* your response to it.

"Visualize or imagine these roots like the veins of rivers, that touch every part and place on earth—Europe, Asia, Africa, the Americas, all islands and the poles. The roots intertwine throughout the earth while the branches shelter the entire planet."

Move into the roots of the Tree. Dive down, reach throughout this vast network and explore.

The roots are anchored in and anchor you to Mother Earth, feeding you just as they feed the Tree. As you breathe in and receive what the Great Mother is giving you, know the depth of your connection to this Mothering Source who holds you secure within Her network of roots. Let your body feel its connection to Her and to earth.

You may sense a place within this network that feels like your own. You have a root (route) that connects you to the Tree in a special way. This is yours alone and will feel very comfortable to you. Look for it now and once you find it, rest there. **"This is the root/route for your life, the source for your individual life."**

Explore your root—its shape, circumference and placement within the underground system of the Tree.

Each time you practice this meditation your root/route and your connection to all other roots will be strengthened. Since every person connects to the Tree of Life via its roots, **"It is impossible to help yourself without benefiting everyone. As you strengthen your root/route, everyone's connection to the Divine gets stronger."**

The Tree exercise is helpful to men and women but something special happens for women when they work with it. For many years women have been cut off from the source of feminine power, and one way to access this power is to work with the Tree of Life. The Grandmothers say, **"It is time for women's roots to be established; the roots of the Tree are like women who stand steady and supportive in their power.**

"As women work with the roots of the Tree of Life each root will reach out and touch another. Together these will form a web of support that will hold the earth steady. This is another way for people to open to the Net of Light."

FRUITS OF THE TREE

"Each fruit is necessary for the overall health of the Tree"

"In human lives and in the Tree of Life energy travels from the Source, up the root/route and into the body. There it manifests as fruit—the fruits of one's actions and the fruits on the Tree of Life." In both cases, fruit ripens gradually.

This exercise allows us to see ourselves in a new way while honoring our specific gifts and challenges. **"Each fruit is necessary to the overall health of the Tree. It is *this* fruit, chosen from the Tree of Life that gives each life its savor. The fruit on the Tree reflects the special identity of each."**

If we think of our fruit as symbolic of how we live and who we are, we can take the lesson of the Tree to a deeper level. Our lives reflect our individuality. Some of us are achievers, some are contemplators, some are survivors, explorers, evaluators—the list goes on. In time our life will manifest these intrinsic qualities [our gifts, challenges and character], just as fruit will manifest whatever is intrinsic to it (its sweetness, color and texture).

To begin this exercise, follow your usual method for relaxing, then call on the Tree of Life and notice its canopy, laden with fruit of every kind. Hanging from its branches are mangos, bananas, guavas, grapefruit, every fruit imaginable. Walk up to the Tree and be aware of the fruit you select or rather, that which selects you.

Whether or not the significance of your fruit is apparent to you is not important. The fruit is a metaphor for your life, so treat it with respect to see what you can learn from it. The Grandmothers purposefully give "lessons" in this non-linear way to help us sneak up on ourselves.

Once you have chosen or been chosen by your fruit, get to know it. You may be tempted to exchange it for another, but resist temptation and study its color, texture and size. Feel its weight and shape, its smoothness or roughness. Smell it, taste it. Take a sensory inventory.

As you explore, you will more deeply own this fruit, and as you claim your fruit you may also choose to claim the special being that you are. The fruit is a teacher, given to help you value your unique qualities.

"The more you let yourself embody your fruit [the truth of your individual manifestation of being] the more you will step forward into the world to be who and what you are. This particular fruit from the Tree of Life is yours. This particular life is also yours. Your fruit, your life, is a gift from yourself and from the Source itself."

To serve and connect with the great cycle of life, we must own who and what we are. The Tree of Life, a metaphor for God/Source, shows that just as each fruit comes from and is part of the tree, we also come from and are part of God/Source. We, the fruit, belong to the tree.

Once we claim our gift from the Tree, we can live out the fruit of our lives and when we do this we bloom. Anyone who has witnessed a friend "come into her own" knows the thrill of seeing this awakening. This part of the Tree of Life meditation nudges us toward "coming into our own."

Fruit inevitably follows flower, so after you bloom, you bear fruit. Once we become ourselves, own our strengths, flaws and talents, we have something to give back to the world. What we give is determined by the fruit we are given and by what we do with it. The fruits of the Tree represent both the hand we are dealt and how we play it. The saying, "Who you are is God's gift to you, what you become is your gift to God," sums it up.

By living out the truth of our Self, we give back to the Tree of Life and complete the cycle of giving and receiving. **"The Tree of Life supports everything that lives by continuously giving of itself. This medita-**

tion will help you own, and then use the gifts of your particular fruit. Then you too will have something to give to the world."

MEDITATION ON THE FABRIC OF BEING

"You are much more than you have conceived.
You are as the night sky."

This meditation expands consciousness by dissolving fears and the illusion of separation from the Divine, as well as separation from one another. By dissolving false barriers it counteracts loneliness and isolation. Liberating, breaking through constrictive beliefs and mindsets, the Fabric of Being frees us to enjoy an expanded state. This is another symbol the Grandmothers use to teach about the Divine and our relationship to it.

The Fabric of Being breaks us out of the confining identification with our individual problems and our small selves, and moves us into contact with the greater Self. Since it is the sense of separateness from the *whole* of life that creates loneliness and isolation in the first place, here we experience joy. This meditation gives a body/mind understanding of union with the Source and union with each other.

The Grandmothers say, **"You *are* the Fabric of Being. Think of the night sky and let yourself move into the indigo blue of this sky. Here there are many stars and moons and a glow from all of these."**

After you reach a state of relaxation, think of the expansive nighttime panorama of moon and stars. If you live where you can see the stars, walk out your door and look up. If not, think of a time when you did look at the deep blue of the night sky and as you gaze at it with your physical or inner eyes, think of the Grandmothers' statement that you are not separate, but part of it all.

Gently breathe and with each inhalation draw the starry sky into your body, then merge into it as you exhale. As you breathe in, the sky enters you. As you breathe out, you flow into the sky. Continue to breathe like this, and explore this expanse. Let yourself be supported by the firmament; the mantle of sky wraps around you, and as you rest enfolded in it, you touch everything—stars, earth and air. **"You encompass all this,"** the Grandmothers say, **"you are the indigo blue night sky. You surround everything and throb with life. The stars and moons in the sky pulsate within you just as your physical heartbeat echoes inside your physical body."**

Be aware of the sky moving in and out of your body to the rhythm of your breath. The life force of the universe *is* inside us. It is underneath our skin, as well as over and around us, but this exercise will allow you to feel it. As you breathe like this, notice the temperature of your body, the rhythm of your breath and your heartbeat.

"**If you were only your body, if you were only your breath, or your thoughts, you would have no recognition of any of them. But you are much more than any of these and because you are, whenever you turn your consciousness inward, you can be aware of them all. You are much more than you have ever conceived. You are as the night sky. Vast.**

"**We give this meditation to move you beyond the sense of limitation and smallness. The Fabric of Being will move you beyond mental divisions of 'me' or 'mine,' 'you' or 'yours.' These are tiny concepts—not even pinpoints—and are not what you are. You are great; you are the deep blue, ever-reaching blanket of the night sky.**

"**Meditating on the Fabric of Being will heal worry, nervousness and release stress. It releases negative mental and emotional states because the Fabric of Being is the truth of who you are.**"

MEDITATION ON THE ROSE OF THE HEART

"This is the jewel of the exercises—the Rose of the Heart."

When this work with the Grandmothers was finished I asked them for a meditation on opening the heart to place at the very end of the book. The Rose of the Heart is an appropriate finish for these exercises.

Since this meditation was dictated to the reader, I will give it in the Grandmothers' words, with phrases or comments of my own inserted only when necessary. Your experience will be deepened if you observe a real rose the first time you do this meditation. Though not essential, it will give you a sensory memory from which to relate.

The Grandmothers say, "**Begin by sensing the center of your chest. What we are doing is, as you say, a 'before and after.' This is the before. Notice the texture of this area of your body, the temperature, softness or hardness, perhaps the color you sense inside your chest. Observe what it is like in the heart area of your body. What is it like?**

"**Get a rose so that you can look at it. Not a tight bud nor one that is fully blown open, but a multi-petaled rose, partially opened.**"

[As they said this they showed me the color range they wanted—somewhere in the spectrum of peaches, pinks and reds.] **"Look into the rose and take your time, smell it. A natural rose that has not been hybridized will have a scent. These are best because scent is intrinsic to the rose.**

"Feel the skin, the petals, of the rose and smell it again as you examine the intricacy of its petals. How beautiful these petals are. Study how each relates to each. Observe the pattern that lies on top and underneath, as well as the petal's delicate edge. Notice how the rose circles round, folding and enfolding, right to the very heart of itself.

"Dissecting a rose will not show you what a rose is because a rose is formed in relation to its petals. The miracle of the rose exists because of its scent, texture, its variation of color and the relationship of its petals.

"How perfect this flower is. How perfect you are. If you only knew! Every part of you relating perfectly to every other—your organs, in harmonious conversation with each other, your essence permeating throughout. Like the rose, the human body can also be dissected; the personality can be dissected and diagnosed. But your essence, which is within every part of you, cannot be touched. As is the rose, so are you.

"Now close your eyes and focus on the heart area of your body. Again notice how it feels, what the sensation is like here and then think of bringing the rose, the beautiful rose you have been studying, into your heart. The rose is now within your heart.

"Watch as it opens slowly. Opening...opening. As you inhale, the rose opens as if it is stretching, and as you breathe out, the rose also breathes out and closes a bit. Breathing in, it opens further, breathing out it closes a little. And at the next breath it opens more, casting its fragrance into the atmosphere.

"As the rose opens, so does your heart. With your in-breath, both the rose and your heart open, with the out-breath they close a little and in the next in-breath they open further. Because the rose/heart follows your breath, this gradual process serves to expand your heart. Breathe now with the rose of your heart, opening a little more each time you inhale.

"Next, expand the rose so that your chest is contained within its petals. Experience this enormous rose of your heart. Now the rose swells throughout your body until it contains your entire body. Feel yourself surrounded by and filled with the rose.

"Expand it further to fill the room you are sitting in and further still to fill the area where you live. Let it expand to saturate your part of the country.

"This enormous heart/rose is now expanding to fill your entire country. Onward, outward, ever outward, it is filling all the countries of the world, holding all the peoples, all bodies of water and landmasses of the earth. The great heart/rose now holds the earth within its petals and expands on until the sun is contained within it, the galaxy, and the universe. Everything. Everything is now contained within your enormous heart/rose.

"Far into space this vast rose of your heart expands until it holds and contains everything. Feel this. Sense this." Rest in this place for a moment and notice what it is like for you to be in such an expanded state before you continue.

"Now the return journey begins, a much faster journey. The Rose of the Heart is beginning its return to you. It is coming in now; it is rushing back, contracting back to your country, to your city, to your home, contracting into your body and last of all, into your own physical heart.

"Take a moment to rest in this space within your heart and observe this area of your body. This is where the rose/heart lives and will always live.

Notice if any changes have occurred since we began this exercise. What is this area of your body like now? How does it feel here in your heart?" Notice the size of your heart, its weight, its temperature, color and texture. Compare your heart now to the way it felt before you did this exercise.

"Such is the beauty and massive magnificence of your own heart," the Grandmothers say. "**Rest here.**"

ABOUT THE AUTHOR

Sharon McErlane has been a teacher and a marriage and family counselor for more than three decades. Her work focuses on teaching clients and students techniques for spiritual and emotional integration, which guide them on their path through life. She teaches Shamanic journeying classes, and travels the world speaking to groups spreading the Grandmothers' message.

She is also an accomplished artist and gardener and has created a graceful environment in her home and garden that many of her students consider a sacred space, and a nurturing environment for her workshops.

She is married with two grown children, and lives with her husband and golden retriever in Laguna Beach, California.

Closing Note from the Author

My work with the Grandmothers continues; whenever they give me a new lesson, I call people together and pass it on. Now people all over the world are sharing the Grandmothers' message with one another. They awaken to the holiness that lives at their core, they feel a loving connection with one another and with the Divine. Many people are now spreading the Grandmothers' Empowerment. A listing of empowerment groups is located on our website at: grandmothersspeak.com.

I do not know where the Grandmothers' work will take me next, but the journey with them has been so enriching that I have vowed to go wherever they lead, and since they do not appear to be finished with me, there is a second book in process, *The Net of Light: Journeys with the Grandmothers* available Spring of 2007.

Working with the Grandmothers has brought me untold joy and I hope that reading about and working with them has given you joy too. This book is offered with love. I am delighted to have been part of their work.

— *Sharon McErlane*